THE TERRIBLE THING THAT HAPPENS

I0630554

CARLTON MELLICK III

ERASERHEAD PRESS
PORTLAND, OREGON

ERASERHEAD PRESS
P.O. BOX 10065
PORTLAND, OR 97296

WWW.ERASERHEADPRESS.COM

ISBN: 978-1-62105-224-1

Also by
Carlton Mellick III

AUTHOR'S NOTE

I've been trying to write a book a month every month this year. It's not something I expect to accomplish, but I like to challenge myself this way, especially since I've been falling behind on my quarterly release schedule lately. I already did this with my books *Exercise Bike*, *Spider Bunny*, and *Every Time We Meet at the Dairy Queen Your Whole Fucking Face Explodes*. All of these were done at a beach house on the Oregon coast, written within week-long writing marathons. Some people think writing a book in a week is insane, but it's really not that difficult, especially if you're writing a 20,000-30,000 word novella. You just need to make sure to write at least 3,000 words a day and pretty much anyone can do that as long as they actually sit down and do the work without going online or giving up when they get stuck. Pretty much everyone I've gone on writing marathons with have been able to accomplish at least 30,000 words in a week. When I wrote *The Terrible Thing That Happens*, I went with bizarro author Vince Kramer. He'd never done a marathon before and hadn't been able to finish a new book in a couple of years, yet he was able to write 7,000 words a day, which was far more than I am typically able to do. Like me, he plans to write books exclusively during writing marathons from now on.

The first day of a writing marathon, I typically go out for drinks and brainstorm my book. When I started this book, I didn't even know what it was going to be about. I went to a bar with Vince and tried to figure out which book I was going to write. I had the idea for a book called Fruit Box about a group of people trapped inside of a children's cereal commercial, but Vince wasn't all that excited about the idea. Whenever I write a book with another writer, I always bounce my ideas off of them. If they don't react in a positive way I won't use my ideas. So I scrapped my original idea and looked over my notes. I have lists of thousands of story ideas on my computer, but choosing the right one is rarely easy to do. When I threw out the idea for a story called Open 24 Hours, about a haunted grocery store in the post apocalypse, Vince got really excited about it. If you know Vince Kramer, he's somebody who wears his emotions on his sleeve. If he hates something, you'll know. If he loves something, you'll know. When it was obvious that he loved the concept, I decided to write this one. But both of us were in agreement that the title had to go.

I spent the rest of the night trying to come up with the right title. I won't ever start a book unless I have at least a working title that I like, because sometimes a good title will encourage me to write a good book. Vince and I brainstormed titles all night. We came up with things like The Last Grocery Store, The Last Shopping Spree, Fallout Market, Plague Market, and Beyond Thunder Mart. But nothing appealed to us. I settled on Plague Market and used that as a working title, but it didn't feel right after a few days so I changed it to The Last Grocery Store, which was boring but suitable. The Terrible Thing That Happens didn't come to me until the end, but I feel like it's the perfect title. This book is meant to have a children's book feel to it, and this title is the only one that worked in that way. In fact, every person who has heard this book title has asked if it's a children's book, so I feel it's the best option.

Besides being a children's book version of a post-apocalypse story, this book is also meant to be a parody of the ghost story genre. I absolutely love ghost stories, especially in film. But, to be honest, I kind of have a problem with ghost movies. Why is it that just because a person dies they automatically gain super human powers? Ghosts have the ability to fly, walk through walls, teleport anywhere, possess people, control dolls, create illusions, change temperatures, pull kids through televisions, shoot beams of ectoplasmic energy from their eyes, they can find anyone anywhere no matter how well they hide, can become invisible whenever they want, they have super human strength and are masters of telekinesis. They also happen to be completely indestructible unless their remains are discovered and properly buried. So what's so special about dying that gives spirits all of these crazy powers? Is there some kind of afterlife wizard school they attend? And since they get such amazing powers after death, why don't ghosts ever use those powers for good instead of just to torment some lame family? They could become world-saving superheroes with all those ghost abilities. And also, how come when a ghost kills a guy he doesn't just kick that ghost's ass once he arrives in the spirit world? They'd have the same ghost abilities (unless he needs to attend afterlife wizard school first). And even if ghosts couldn't hurt each other that guy could just use his find-anything-anywhere ability to locate the ghost's remains, teleport over to them, then telekinesis the bones onto hallowed ground. Movie over in ten minutes.

This book focuses on an equally absurd concept involving a haunting, but it's not the ghosts that are the absurd part. It is the location. Although the book is not a comedy, the idea of a people in a post-apocalyptic wasteland surviving solely on food from a haunted grocery store made me smile. But, to tell you the truth, I don't think I ever would have had the guts to actually write it if it wasn't for Vince Kramer's enthusiasm. So if you happen to like this one you have Vince to thank. I hope you enjoy it.

—Carlton Mellick III, 5/28/2016, 7:14am

CHAPTER ONE
CHOCKY

The hills were made of bone and metal. They stretched as far as the eye could see, twisting the landscape into a grotesque maze of debris and wreckage. It was a bustling city once. Long, long ago. A place where millions of souls jittered with life. Now it's a flattened graveyard, rusting beneath the ever-black sky.

As he climbed through the ruins, Chocky knew it was pointless. He knew nothing could survive on the surface anymore, not for another hundred years. There was no food, no water, no life of any kind. But he had nowhere else to go. He couldn't go back home. There was nothing left to go back to. All he could do was move forward, counting down the seconds until he finally met his fate.

The ground was jagged and sharp, cutting his leather boots to muddy shreds. His soft feet were bruised and bleeding, infected with irradiated dust. The mask he wore did little to protect him from the toxic atmosphere, the filters all worn out. His eyes were swollen and red. He choked and gagged on every breath he took.

As he continued forward, Chocky could barely see

where he placed his steps. The last batteries in his last source of light were fading. Once gone, he would be in complete darkness. He wasn't sure if it was day or night. The sun had been covered in clouds of ash for decades. Once the batteries died, he'd have no way to recharge them. He would not be able to see even his hands in front of his face and could continue no farther.

When the flashlight began flickering, he knew it wouldn't be much longer.

"At least I got to see the surface…" Chocky said to the dimming light.

He had been underground his whole life, always curious about the big world above. He never thought he'd actually get a chance to see it in his lifetime. He was told that with luck his great grandchildren would return to the surface one day and reclaim the Earth. But that was no longer a possibility. He wasn't going to have great grandchildren. Nobody was. Unless there was another bunker out there, somewhere in the world, the human race would die with him.

When the light went out, flickering its last flicker, Chocky fell to his knees and removed his mask. He closed his eyes tight and breathed in the toxic atmosphere as deeply as he could, hoping that it wouldn't take too long to kill him.

But as he opened his eyes, the landscape wasn't completely dark. There was a light in the distance. He coughed the ash from his lungs, rubbed it from his eyes, and looked again. The light was still there. He was sure it wasn't there before. It couldn't have been.

"What in the world are you?" he said to the new light.

He put the mask over his face, got to his feet, and hiked in the direction of the twinkling brightness. Unable to see the ground below him, he tripped several times as he hiked through the rubble. But he didn't care about a few scrapes and bruises. He had to find out what could possibly be generating such a light.

"Could it be people?" he asked the rubble he stomped upon. "Could anyone be alive up here after all this time?"

He knew that it was impossible. He was told over and over again that nobody could survive on the surface. The atmosphere was toxic, the temperatures below freezing, the water undrinkable, food could not grow. The light had to be something else. A glowing mineral deposit, maybe. Or a natural gas fire. Maybe it was even a mere delusion. Whatever it was, Chocky wouldn't let himself die until he found out for sure.

When he was close enough to make out the source of the light, Chocky couldn't believe his eyes. A glowing sign that read "Super Foods" illuminated the landscape, and beyond the sign was a grocery store. Surrounded by miles and miles of rubble, the building still stood. It was perfectly intact, completely untouched by the devastation that took place over fifty years ago. Chocky had seen the same kind of grocery store in movies before. It looked exactly as it did in those ancient dramas from the old world. It appeared to be in perfect condition, clean and new, not blemished by even a speck of the dust that coated everything else in the wasteland.

As Chocky stepped into the parking lot, he figured it had to be some kind of trick. There was no way it was actually real. There was no electricity to power it, nothing to keep it so spotless. He looked into the windows. The place was even brighter and cleaner within. The shelves were fully stocked with more varieties of foods than Chocky had ever seen in his life. It was a secret oasis. A miraculous paradise.

"Am I dead?" Chocky asked. "Is this Heaven?"

The doors opened for him as he stepped up to the entrance. Warm air hit his skin as he stepped in from the cold. He removed his mask, brushed the dust from his face and clothes. The air inside was fresh, breathable. His bloody feet tracked red prints across the tile floor.

When the door closed behind him, Chocky finally believed it—the place was actually real. He was not dead. It was not an illusion. There was no possible explanation for it, but there it was. The place was a miracle.

There were no other people in sight, just aisles and aisles of freshly packaged products. He went toward the closest food he could see, right into the produce section. The scent of fresh fruit was strong and pleasing. He picked up the closest piece of fruit he could grab—a bright red apple. When he bit into it, moisture exploded into his dusty dried-out mouth. The flavor was tart and sweet. He'd never tasted anything like it before.

There were so many fruits he'd never tasted before. Grapes, kiwis, oranges, cucumbers, pineapple, blueberries.

The hydroponic garden that grew fruits and vegetables underground had only a few varieties, and he rarely ate them when they were fresh. He had no idea where all of these fruits could have possibly come from, where they could have possibly been grown.

He went from fruit to fruit, tasting every single one. Even though they burned the sores in his mouth with their potent acids, the flavors were so powerful and delicious that he couldn't stop shoveling them down his throat.

"Oh, God…" he moaned as he bit into a mango. Even though he bit through the bitter peeling, the insides of the fruit were the most delectable of any he'd tasted so far. He ripped off the skin and sucked on the squishy yellowish-orange meat. He put three into his pockets, then moved on to the papayas.

Chocky was so busy tasting everything he could find that he didn't realize the woman standing behind him. It wasn't until he turned around, to go toward the berries, that he saw her.

The sight of her made him jump back and drop all the lemons and grapefruit in his arms. In her clean blue dress, with matching high heeled shoes, she was dressed like a woman from the old world. Her dyed red hair was styled into a short bob that curled into her neck. Red nail polish painted her fingers and toes. She carried a shopping basket, filling it with fresh produce—leeks, rainbow chard, portabella mushrooms, and sweet Hawaiian onions—casually shopping at the grocery store as though gathering ingredients for a dinner party.

He was frozen in his place by the sight of her, unable

to blink or make a sound. She was the most beautiful woman Chocky had ever seen. In the underground bunker, women and men did not look much different from each other. They wore the same clothes, had the same hair styles. There was no makeup or nail polish, no hair dyes or fancy dresses. This woman looked just like the ones from the movies, the ones the young women idolized, the ones young men drooled over. Chocky always thought of them as mere fantasies, not real human beings. But there the woman was, standing before him, as real as the fruit he'd just eaten.

Chocky wondered if he'd been transported back in time. He'd seen several time travel movies in his life. When he was a child, he always dreamed of building a time machine and being transported back to the days when the world was bright and wonderful. Once he was old enough to realize traveling through time was an absolute impossibility, he gave up on his dream. But at that moment, he thought maybe, just maybe, he had somehow accomplished traveling back in time as he'd always wished.

When he looked back and saw the black devastated world outside the store's windows, he realized that he was wrong. He was not in the past. But perhaps this store had been transported through time from the past.

The woman in the blue dress walked past Chocky to get to the limes. As she neared, her flowery perfume overwhelmed him, made him feel light and dizzy. He must have smelled like a sewage tank compared to her.

"Umm… hello?" he asked her as she passed.

She didn't seem to hear him.

He glanced at the entrance of the store and then back at the woman. He had to warn her about the outside world. If she had been transported to his world she didn't know the danger she was in.

"Do you know where you are?" Chocky asked, stepping toward her.

She ignored him. He wondered if she ignored him on purpose. He was so out of place in her world. She must have thought he was some kind of deranged homeless man, like the ones in old movies that everyone used to despise and avoid.

"My name is Chocky. Do you know where you are?"

She didn't respond. He moved closer to her.

"Hello?" he asked.

She said nothing.

Then he yelled louder. "Hello?"

She squeezed the limes one at a time, completely oblivious to Chocky.

He yelled right in her ear, "Why won't you talk to me?"

She was completely unfazed by it. She put a lime in her cart and then went toward the bakery section of the store.

Chocky followed her, getting right in front of her and waving his hands in her face. She did not respond. It was like she did not even see him. He was invisible to her. It was like he was a ghost.

"What's going on?" he asked her.

But she just continued shopping.

There were other shoppers in the store apart from the woman. A young man with a well-manicured beard. A mother with two children. An old married couple. A few giggling teenage girls. All of them were like the woman. They all were dressed like people of the old world, all shopping like it were the most normal thing to do in the post-apocalyptic world.

"Hello?" Chocky called out to the store. "Can anyone hear me?"

But none of them responded.

"Anyone? Please?"

He could hear them when the shoppers spoke to each other. The mother scolded her children for knocking boxes of cereal off the shelves. The old woman discussed the rising prices of soup with her husband. But they could not hear Chocky. He felt as afraid and alone as he had on the surface.

But then there was a commotion on the other side of the store…

"Let's go!" someone cried, a man's voice. "We're out of time!"

When Chocky looked in the direction of the shouting, he saw two people just as out of place as he was. They were filthy vagabonds. Dirt and ash covered their faces and ragged clothing. Fabric was wrapped around their mouths, goggles over their eyes. They had shopping carts filled to the top of with groceries, racing through the store at top speed.

When they passed Chocky, the male vagabond yelled at him, "Time's up. Move your ass."

Chocky couldn't believe it. The guy could see him. He even spoke to him.

The female vagabond looked back at Chocky and said, "Wait a minute… Who the hell is that?"

She stopped her cart and looked directly at him.

Chocky didn't understand. "Wait… you can see me?"

"He's not from here," she says to her friend. "Where the hell did he come from?"

The male shook his head. "Who cares. We're out of time." Then he continued on his way.

The woman looked back, her dreadlocked hair dangling in her face.

"Whoever you are, you better get out of here. It's not safe."

Chocky didn't know what she meant. He looked back. The young man with the beard was right next to them, scanning a display of expensive beer. He didn't seem to acknowledge the grubby woman right next to him. He didn't seem afraid or anxious in the slightest.

"I don't understand," Chocky asked. "What is this place?"

Before the woman could speak, there was a loud booming noise. The bearded man's head exploded, blood and bits of brain splattered against my chest.

As the man's body hit the ground, the grubby woman cried, "They're here!"

Then she turned and ran.

Chocky looked beyond the dead man's body and

saw something coming down the aisle toward him. It was a large man with a brown paper bag over his head. An angry face was drawn with crayon on the front of the mask, with holes for eyes so that he could see. He pumped his shotgun and fired again, blowing the legs out from under the old man as his wife screamed and knocked dozens of cans of tomato soup onto the floor.

Chocky ducked and ran. He hurried in the direction of the filthy people, following their trail of ashy footprints across the ceramic floor.

Screams and gunfire erupted all around him as Chocky ran. More people with guns marched through the store with rifles and shotguns, wearing paper bags and cardboard boxes over their faces.

As Chocky ran for the exit, the two vagrants stood outside the doors, waving him toward them.

"Come on, come on!" they shouted.

Chocky looked back and saw the woman with the blue dress cowering against a shelf of freshly baked breads, holding her basket of vegetables against her like it was her own crying baby. The man with the shotgun came up behind her, pointing the barrel of the gun against the back of her head. She didn't see him. She wasn't going to be able to run away in time. She was going to die.

"Look out!" Chocky yelled.

When he said this, the woman looked up. She looked right at Chocky, as though she heard him, as though she could now see him with her very own eyes.

Somebody grabbed Chocky from behind.

"Come on," the filthy woman said.

She pulled him back. Chocky resisted. He couldn't leave the woman in the blue dress behind. He had to save her somehow.

But he was weak from going days without food or water. He didn't have any fight left in him. The filthy woman easily overpowered him, yanking him out of the exit. The second his foot hit the pavement of the parking lot, the store went black. The lights went out. The sound of screaming faded.

"What the hell are you doing?" Chocky said to the two vagrants in the darkness. "We have to go back. We have to save them."

The woman pushed him.

"Are you crazy?" she said. "Are you a crazy person? You could have gotten yourself killed."

"But all those people…"

"What people?" The woman turned on a flashlight and shined it into the store.

There was nothing inside anymore. The building was in ruins, burned out and filled with rubble. There were no people, no food, nothing but ash and decay, just like the rest of the wasteland.

"There's no one inside of there," she said. "All the people you saw died a long, long time ago."

CHAPTER TWO
PICKLE

Chocky stepped into the ruins of the grocery store. He couldn't believe it. None of it was real. But when he felt his pockets, the mangos he had taken were still inside. He pulled one out, felt it in his hand. It was just as real as the clothes on his back.

Looking at the vagabonds' grocery carts filled with food and products, they too were real. He had no idea why the grocery store disappeared but the groceries did not.

"Where did you come from?" the woman asked. "Who are you?"

Chocky didn't respond, too focused on the ruins and the groceries to speak.

"You're not from Subway. Are you from Station? I thought the disease killed everyone there."

Chocky shook his head. "No, I walked here from the south. About five days away."

"That's impossible," the man said. "There isn't anything that far from Store."

Chocky didn't care about explaining where he came from. He was more curious about what had just transpired.

"What was that place?" he asked. "Why did it disappear like that?"

The man picked a flashlight out of his grocery cart and took it out of the package. He inserted batteries, turned it on, and shined it in Chocky's face.

"Maybe he's delirious," the man said. "The disease from Station makes people delirious."

"I don't think he's from Station," the woman said.

"I think we should leave him, anyway," the man said, a stern yet worried tone in his voice. "If he has the disease he'll infect us all."

The woman shook her head. "He doesn't have the disease. He'd have lumps and his skin would be green." She stepped closer to Chocky. "I think he's telling the truth."

She removed the hood from Chocky's head and got a good look at him. "He doesn't have any defects."

"We should leave him anyway," the man said.

She shook her head. "No, he's special. I'm bringing him home."

"Are you crazy?" the man asked.

But she ignored him. She looked at Chocky and removed her goggles, revealing two large bulging froglike eyes. When she blinked, Chocky stepped back.

"I'm Pickle," she told him, cocking her head. "My brother here is called Radishes."

"I'm Chocky."

She looked back at her brother. For some reason, just by the mere sight of Chocky, the man was finally convinced.

"Nice to meet you, Chocky," she says, smiling with pointed teeth. "Now let's get out of the ash. We can talk more once we're safe."

Pickle and Radishes led Chocky down a narrow path through the hills of wreckage, pushing their rattling carts in front of them. Less than a mile down, they came to the edge of a vast crater. They took out all of their groceries and stuffed them into large yellow duffel bags. Pickle handed two of them to Chocky and told him to carry them for her. Then they pushed the empty carts over the side.

When Chocky looked over the edge, he saw a vast sea of grocery carts. There were thousands upon thousands of them. Some were brand new, like the ones they just pushed off, but others were old and rusted. It was as though these people had been disposing their carts in this pit for decades.

"This way," Pickle said.

She led him toward a wide cavern opening in the side of a mountain of concrete debris. Twenty feet inside, they opened a large gate with sheets of metal welded to its front, acting as some kind of barrier of protection from the outside world. They closed the gate behind them and descended into what was once a vast subway system. They stepped down a staircase which looked to once have been an escalator, several decades ago.

"Your people survived down here all this time?"

Chocky asked, removing his mask and hood.

Pickle nodded. "We were here in Subway. Our grandparents' grandparents survived the Great Disaster by hiding in this place. Without Subway and Store, we would not be alive."

It was warm in the old subway. Fires in metal barrels lined their path, heating the decrepit tunnels. There were over three hundred people living down there, huddling together in small shacks made of debris from the surface.

Strange people stared at Chocky as Pickle and Radishes escorted him down the old subway tracks. They had never seen an outsider like him before.

"Who's that, why is he here?" they asked each other, but they wouldn't go anywhere near him.

All the people were ratty and deformed like Pickle. Some of them were even worse than she. They had twisted faces, growths on their heads, pointed ears or no ears at all. One of them had a long tail growing from her back. One had tiny arms the size of a baby's. One had eyes sunken deep into his skull. One had only a single large eye in the center of her face.

The toxic atmosphere had done something to the people surviving in the subway town. They didn't have it as good as Chocky did growing up in the bunker. They all suffered from horrific birth defects. All of them were very young, twenty-five at the oldest. Life expectancy in the subway wasn't as good as the bunker, where people lived at least three times that length.

When Pickle saw all the people staring at them, a worried look crossed her face.

"We need to get you inside," she told Chocky. "Our home is just ahead."

She took him by the hand and pulled him through the gathering mutants. But before she could get them home, a small group of the freakish women blocked their way. They were led by a large woman with swollen lips and three fat misshapen breasts.

"What do we have here?" said the woman in a deep, growling voice. She was more animal than human, like a warthog standing on two feet.

"Stay away from him, Eggs," Pickle told her.

The beastly woman squinted her eyes, which were spread too far apart on her face. "He's quite a specimen, isn't he?" She grabbed Chocky's cheeks with her fat walrus fingers and moved his head to the side, examining him. "He seems almost completely… pure."

"Get away," Pickle said, pulling Chocky back. "He's not for you."

"He's open for the choosing, isn't he?" Eggs said. "Just like all the other men…"

Pickle shook her head. "Not this one."

Eggs turned her attention to Pickle. She grabbed her by her ragged ashy clothes and leaned in close. "And why the hell not?"

"I took him from Store," Pickle said. "You know the rules. Anything I take from Store belongs to me. He's my property."

"That rule doesn't apply to people," said Eggs.

"Says who?" Pickle said. "Nobody has ever taken a person from Store."

Then she pushed past the group of women and pulled Chocky close behind her.

"Napkin will hear about this," Eggs said, grumbling under her breath.

But Pickle didn't respond. She took Chocky and her brother to their home, three shacks down, and locked the door firmly behind them with three latches and a deadbolt.

The inside of the shack was small and smelled of festering garbage. Empty cans and food wrappers littered the rubber carpet. A smoldering fire pit centered the room.

"What was that?" Chocky asked Pickle. "Why did you say I was your property?"

Pickle took off her goggles. Her bugging eyes glared at him, annoyed by his words. "I said that to save you."

When Radishes took off his goggles and hood, Chocky realized that he looked similar to his sister. He had the same tiny pointed teeth and bulging frog eyes of his sister. But his nose was much different. It was smooth and flat, with two tiny nostrils blowing little bubbles of air. They removed their gloves, revealing webbed froglike fingers.

"Pickle did you a favor," Radishes said. "Eggs would have mated you if she didn't say that."

"Mated me?"

Pickle was surprised by his ignorance. "Men have freedom to refuse mating where you come from?"

Chocky shrugged, not quite sure what she meant.

Pickle explained it to him, "In Subway, women have

the right to mate any man she chooses. Men are not allowed to refuse. It is one of our rules here."

"Why can't men refuse?"

"The rule was created many years ago," Pickle said. "In the beginning, men and women formed couplings, where only a single woman could mate with each man. But there were far more women than there were men. It wasn't fair. Our people decided to outlaw couplings, so that all women can mate with whichever partner they choose. Men lost the right to refuse a woman's mating request. Because women want to mate with the healthiest males, it isn't right for men to be particular with who they seed."

"That doesn't seem fair to the men," Chocky said.

"But it's important to the future of our species."

Pickle licked her lips. The way she looked at him with her bugged out eyes worried Chocky. By their laws, he could be forced to mate with her if she decided she wanted him to. He hoped that being an outsider meant he wasn't bound by their laws.

"But isn't it bad for the future of your species?" Chocky asked.

"How could it be bad?" Pickle asked.

"If there's one male that is healthier and more attractive than all the other males, then all the women would choose to mate with him," Chocky said. "Then all of that generation's children would be fathered by one man. It's bad for the gene pool."

Pickle shrugged off Chocky's argument. She asked, "How do your people mate then? Do you have the right to refuse?"

Chocky shook his head. "Not exactly."

"What do you mean?" Pickle asked.

"Our mates are chosen by a computer program," Chocky said. The two of them nodded, but didn't seem to understand what a computer program was. "My people also created a rule to protect the future of our species, but we didn't outlaw couplings. Couples were chosen by a computer to create the strongest offspring. It was designed to ensure a healthy and long-lasting gene pool."

"So women can't choose who to mate?" Pickle asked with a confused and disturbed face. "That sounds barbaric."

"It's not any worse than our system," said Radishes.

Pickle asked, "Do you have a mate where you come from?"

"I did, but..." Chocky looked down. "She died. Everyone died."

"How?" Pickle asked. "Did the disease get them?"

Chocky shook his head. "There was an explosion. I think one of the reactor's failed. The bunker was flooded with radiation. I'm the only one who escaped in time."

"So there really were other people out there?" asked Radishes. "People who survived without Store? We were told no such people exist."

"Store?" Chocky asked. "You mean that grocery store we were in?"

They nodded their heads.

"What was that place?" Chocky asked. "I don't understand how it could be there one minute and disappear the next."

"It's always been like that," Pickle said. "It's been there for a very long time, even before the Great Disaster."

"But what is it?"

"It's a haunted place," Pickle said. "Everything and everyone there are all ghosts."

Chocky pulled out a mango and held it up. "But this isn't a ghost? I can hold it in my hands. I can eat it."

Pickle just ignored the mango, unable to explain it.

She continued, "Something terrible happened there. A whole store full of people were massacred, killed by a group of men in masks. Nobody survived. When something as terrible as that happens, it creates a haunting. The event has been stained on time itself and repeats itself every night at the exact same moment that it took place."

"When we enter Store, we become a part of their world," said Radishes. "We can interact with the haunting. We can gather groceries and bring them from their world to ours."

Pickle opened a yellow duffel bag and lifted a handful of food products. She showed him a box of Twinkies, a package of hamburger meat, a bag of mini candy bars, a pack of steak knives, some cans of pineapple juice.

She said, "Store's inventory is replenished every night, so we have a never-ending supply of fresh food and clean water. Our people have survived for years by taking food from Store."

"But you can't stay in there for very long," Radishes said. "Store is both a blessing and a curse. It might have ensured our survival, but it's also very dangerous. If you stay inside of Store for too long you won't be able to escape."

Pickle nodded at her brother's words. "You become

a part of Store. You get trapped in the Vortex."

"What's the Vortex?" Chocky asked.

"It is the place Store goes after it disappears," Pickle said. "If you don't leave Store before a certain time, you become a part of it. You become one of the victims. You will no longer be invisible to the people inside. The men in masks will murder you with all the others."

"Many of our people have been trapped in the Vortex," said Radishes. "Only one of them has ever survived."

"A man named Cocoa and his friends were drunk on red wine while inside of Store and lost track of time," Pickle said. "When the men in masks came, they couldn't get out. Cocoa survived by hiding behind the deli, but he watched his friends all get shot down like the other ghosts in the store. He was stuck there for twenty-four hours before the Vortex finally set him free. The store was reset and he was able to walk out. But his friends were gone. Their bodies just disappeared with all the other ghosts, vanishing into the vortex."

"If Pickle didn't pull you out in time you would have been stuck in the vortex yourself," said Radishes. "You're lucky she's such a nice person."

Pickle smiled at Chocky, hoping to receive his gratitude for saving his life as she did. But Chocky ignored Radishes' words and shook his head at them.

"I don't buy it," he told them. "How could the simple act of massacring a group of people cause such a thing to occur? There have been massacres far worse than that one throughout history and nothing like that has ever happened before. Even the Great Disaster, as you call it, is a far worse event. How come the entire world isn't as haunted as that grocery store? How come all the cities on the planet don't go back to what they were once like at the same time every day like what happens at Super Foods?"

The two of them shrugged at him.

"I don't know," Pickle said. "Nobody knows. But it happens. There's no other explanation for it."

The shack was only one room, the size of a small living room, but separated into four sections: Pickle's sleeping area, Radishes' sleeping area, a food storage/preparation area, and the main living space. The sleeping areas mostly consisted of homemade beds—the sheets were made from sewn together Super Foods employee T-shirts, as were the mattresses and pillows, only the shirts were stuffed with hundreds of cotton balls before they were sewn together. They stacked grocery baskets together to form makeshift dressers, where they stored their clothes and personal belongings. Everything in their home was made out of objects they collected from Super Foods. Even the couches were constructed out of packages of paper towels and toilet paper wrapped in garbage bags and placed onto the frames of grocery carts.

After eating four apples and two bananas, Radishes went to sleep in his section of the shack, curled up with a stuffed bunny that was so scuffed up that he must have been sleeping with it since he was a small child. Chocky wondered if his mother got the bunny for him from Super Foods when he was young. He wondered if he still slept with it because it reminded him of her.

Pickle stayed up with Chocky, eating Twinkies and fresh plums. She didn't offer to share any food with him, but he had his own mangos that he could eat.

"Since your people are dead, you can live with us if you want," Pickle said, her frog lips sticky with plum juice. "But you'll most likely have to obey our laws, which means I won't be able to protect you from Eggs or the other women here."

Chocky shivered at the thought of being with that Eggs woman. In fact, the idea of sleeping with any of the women he had seen so far, even Pickle, disturbed him. He could tell Pickle liked him. She probably wouldn't have let him stay with them if she didn't. But he couldn't imagine making love to the froglike woman. He was thankful she was nice enough not to force him into it. With their laws, she could have. He would have had to decide between that and finding another shelter someplace else, out in the wasteland.

"I'm not sure if I'm going to stay," Chocky told them.

"Why not?" Pickle asked. "Where else will you go?"

"Maybe I'll find another shelter."

"Like Station?"

"What is Station?"

"It was a place where other survivors lived. They did not like our laws so they would not live in Subway with us. They thought we were gross and dirty. They thought they were more pure than any of us."

"How did they survive?"

"Like us, because of Store. We used to see them in Store, gathering groceries. They didn't speak to us. We didn't speak to them. But eventually, they stopped coming. Nobody has seen them since. Napkin says it was because of disease."

"Who's Napkin?"

"She's our leader. She enforces the rules. We'll have to tell her about you in the morning, when we go to give her tribute. Withholding information from our leader is also against our rules."

"What do you mean by tribute?"

"We have to give her a portion of our groceries," Pickle said. "She is too important to go to Store like everyone else, so we all must bring her tribute so that she won't ever need to."

"So everyone goes to the store when they need food? Nobody stays behind?"

"Some people don't need to. Some are provided for. Children don't go, because their mother goes for them. Our healer, Nail Clippers, rarely has to go because people bring him food in exchange for medical care. Some women, the pretty ones, don't go because they have men bringing food for them, hoping they'll be chosen for a mate session. Some of the old and sickly don't go if they have family who provide for them. But, for the most part, everyone goes to Store at least once per month."

After Pickle went to sleep in her squishy T-shirt bed,

Chocky was left by himself in the living area. He lay on the couch by the crackling fire, thinking about all that happened to him in the past week. He couldn't believe he was still alive. When he escaped the bunker into the wasteland, he assumed he was entering a lifeless world and would soon be a dead man. But there he was, alive and well.

He wasn't sure about the people of Subway or if he wanted to have anything to do with him. He could hear them scurrying outside the shack door, still talking about him in hushed tones. They were freaks. He completely understood why the people of Station refused to associate with them.

For the time being, he would have to put up with the Subwayans. He had to learn all he could about the haunted grocery store. That, not them, was the key to his survival. But it wasn't just the food and supplies he was interested in. He also wanted to see the woman in the blue dress again. If she was a ghost as Pickle and Radishes said, then she would reappear with the grocery store tomorrow night, just as she was when Chocky first saw her.

Chocky thought the woman was so beautiful, far more than any woman he'd ever met. It hurt him to think about the horrible thing that happened to her. He wished she wasn't killed in the massacre. He wished she would survive. He wondered if it was possible to save her from the grocery store, pull her out of it just like he did to the mangos in his belly. Then she would be real and would never have to be killed ever again. He could create a new shelter somewhere else—perhaps at the place called Station, if the people there were truly dead or gone—and bring the woman in the blue dress there. They could live together and create their own society, one with normal people from the old world. He could save more people from Super Foods. The mother and her children. The three teenage girls.

If the fruits were replenished every night, then perhaps the people would be as well. Chocky could take several copies of the woman in the blue dress out of the store, one per night, until he had a dozen of them. Together, they could create a whole new society. They wouldn't have to be ghosts any longer.

Chocky knew that it was not likely possible, but he wanted to entertain the idea for a while longer. It was a much better idea than staying in Subway with all of the inbred mutants.

CHAPTER THREE
NAPKIN

Morning in Subway was different from the night. Although there was no sun to distinguish day from night outside, in the tunnels the mutants lit large lanterns on the ceiling, ones they made themselves out of candles and blue wrapping paper. It was much brighter in the underground than it had been upon Chocky's arrival, which meant he could clearly see the freaks and all of their grotesque deformities.

When he stepped out of the shack with Pickle and Radishes, a crowd formed around them. They all wanted to get a look at the newcomer, the purest man most of them had ever seen. Eggs was there with them. She didn't say anything this time, just watching. They all ogled him with their mouths hanging open, as Pickle led him through the crowd, leading him deeper into the tunnel.

Pickle and Radishes carried all of their duffel bags with them. They were bringing them to Napkin. Even though they got to keep most of their groceries for themselves, their leader got to choose which items would be tribute. She almost always took the best foods from their haul.

"I don't get it," Chocky said. "Why do you have to give anything to the woman just because she's your leader?"

"That's the way it's always been," Pickle said.

"But my people had a leader and he always did twice as much work as anyone else," Chocky said. "He didn't have to do less. And he didn't get anything he didn't work for."

"Napkin is the keeper of our history," Pickle said. "If she were to die in Store then our history would be forgotten. It has to be this way. There's no other choice."

"What if you refused to give her anything?" Chocky asked.

"That is against the rules."

"What if you break the rules?"

"If you break the rules you will be banished from Subway. You will most likely die out in the ash, even if you stayed near Store."

"I'm sure you could find another shelter out there. One like Subway or Station."

"There are no other shelters than Station and Subway."

"Have you looked?"

"No, and I wouldn't want to look. Subway is my home. I don't mind paying tribute to Napkin in order to keep my home."

Napkin's house was also a shack, but it was the biggest of any Chocky had seen. It was the size of a house from the old world, but built of old wooden boards and rusted car parts. When they arrived, Pickle knocked on the door. A young man opened it for her. He was maybe seventeen, muscled and without a shirt. He was much less mutated than the other men in Subway. Although born without ears or hair and his fingers a bit too long for his hands, he wasn't that atrocious-looking.

When brought into the living room of their leader's home, Chocky met who he knew must have been the one called Napkin. She was a massive woman, even larger than Eggs. Her legs and arms were very stubby, too stubby for her body. Her eyes were big like Pickle's, but drooped low on her head. She was one of the more unattractive mutants Chocky had seen. She was also by far the oldest, at about thirty or thirty-five years of age—a dinosaur compared to the rest of her people. Staying underground, out of the toxic atmosphere, her whole life had assisted in her longevity.

Two more young men were sitting on the couch near Napkin. They warmed her with their body heat, feeding her jelly beans from a plastic tray. All of the men were in much better condition than the other freaks in Subway. Napkin must have taken care of them, giving them a portion of the food she received as tribute. Chocky didn't want to think of what they had to do in exchange for the food.

"So this is the one I've been hearing so much about," Napkin said.

"Yes, Napkin," Pickle said, bowing her head in respect.

Napkin looked Chocky in the eyes. "What is your name, new boy?"

"Chocky," he said.

"Chocky?" she asked. "Do you mean Chocolate?"

"No, just Chocky."

Napkin shook her head. "You can't be called Chocky. Nobody will understand that nonsense name. You're to be called Chocolate from now on."

Chocolate looked at Pickle and whispered. "Can she do that? Can she just change my name?"

Pickle nodded at him.

"We have never had visitors such as yourself before," Napkin said. "This is rather new and exciting to us. We thought everyone beyond Store perished many generations ago."

"We thought the same thing," Chocolate said. "I was shocked to find other people alive on the surface. My people always said that survival up here was impossible."

"And where are the rest of your people? Are they friendly? Do they wish to use Store as the people of Station did?"

Pickle spoke for him. "His people are dead now. He's all alone."

Napkin nodded, almost pleased to hear that he had no home.

"I'm sorry to hear that," Napkin said. Then she changed her tone from fake-compassionate to genuinely stern. "Now, onto another matter, Eggs told me she wanted to mate you but you refused her. Is this true?"

Before Chocolate could respond, Pickle said, "He refused because he's my property."

Napkin sighed. "Eggs told me you'd say this. How exactly is he *your* property?"

"I took him from Store," Pickle said. "That makes him mine."

"He's a person," Napkin said. "Not a piece of fruit."

"It doesn't matter," Pickle said. "The rule says that anything I take from Store can't be used by anyone else without my permission."

Napkin shrugged. "Very well. If you claim to treat him as a simple grocery, then I'll accept him as tribute."

"But…" Pickle stuttered and shook her head.

"Those are the rules, aren't they?" Napkin said. "I get to take five items from each of your bounties. If he is one of your items, then I choose him. And all women in Subway will have my permission to use him, all of them but you."

"But…" Pickle tried to argue. "But, no…"

"Unless you're no longer claiming him to be your property?" Napkin asked.

Pickle stepped back and lowered her head. She didn't know what else to say to protect Chocolate. Her excuse would only make it worse for him.

"No, he's not my property," Pickle said. "But I found him in Store. I saved him from the Vortex."

"I see, you feel he owes you for saving his life," Napkin said. "Very well. Since you put your life on the line to save his, I will allow you to mate him before anyone else has the right."

With that, Pickle no longer defended him. She just turned her head and smirked bashfully, her cheeks blushing at the thought.

"I'm not going to mate anyone," said Chocolate.

"Those are the rules, new boy," Napkin said. "You don't have a choice."

"But I haven't decided whether I want to even live

in your community yet," Chocolate said. "For now, I'm just a guest. I don't have to obey your rules."

Napkin paused and looked away for a moment, contemplating his words. There were obviously no rules concerning guests of Subway.

"It doesn't matter," Napkin said. "While you're in Subway, you must obey our laws."

"Why?" Chocolate asked. "If I disobey a rule then I'll just have to leave Subway and never return, but why should I care if I already plan to leave?"

Napkin scrunched her lips and thought about it again. Then she said, "Very well. Since you are new to our laws and customs, you will be allowed a one-week leniency period. You must still pay tribute if you take anything from Store. You must still respect other people's property and well-being. But the women of Subway do not have the right to mate you without your permission. I will make sure of this."

Chocolate was surprised by the woman. She turned out to be far more reasonable than he first expected.

"Thank you," he said.

"But by the end of the seventh day, you must decide. You either become a citizen of Subway and abide by all of its rules, or you must leave."

"I understand," Chocolate said.

"While you're here, I would also like to learn more of your people, for our history. Consider that payment for your shelter."

"Of course," Chocolate said, stepping away.

"And don't worry, Pickle," Napkin added. "If he chooses

to stay you will still have the right to mate him first."

Chocolate moved to the back of the room, waiting for the others. Napkin took her time as she went through their duffel bags, choosing what to keep as her tribute. He watched his new friends groaned and sighed with each item their leader stole from their bags.

While contemplating his future, Chocolate wasn't sure what he was going to do. He didn't want to stay in Subway, especially not if he was to become what basically amounted to a sex slave for a whole race of hideously deformed women. He didn't want any of them. He wanted the woman in the grocery store, the one with the blue dress. He wanted to see if it was possible to take her out of there, make her a part of his world. If he could then he didn't need Subway. He could leave them and wouldn't be bound to any of their rules.

But if he couldn't save the woman, if she wasn't the same as the mangos or any of the other groceries that survived outside of the store, then Chocolate would have no other choice. He'd have to stay in Subway. He'd have to follow their rules.

Looking over at Pickle and her frog-shaped eyes, he cringed at the thought of mating with her. He liked the idea of being her friend. He was even fine with living in her home. He just didn't want her to mother his children. And if Pickle made him cringe, the other mutant women, especially Eggs, made him absolutely repulsed.

When they left Napkin's shack, Eggs was already outside waiting for Chocolate. A hideous grin stretched across her bulbous face.

"Now that that's sorted, you can come with me," Eggs said, grabbing at her lower abdomen as though clutching her womb.

Chocolate shivered.

"You're out of luck, Eggs," Pickle said, stepping in front of Chocolate. "He's off limits for a week."

"What?" Eggs yelled. "What kind of bullshit is this?"

Pickle said, "He's not one of us, so Napkin gave him the right of refusal unless he decides to stay in Subway. He has a week to make up his mind. Until then, you can't mate him."

"Are you kidding me?" Eggs cried, squeezing her fists as though ready to pummel all three of them into the dirt. "I can't wait a week. I'm ovulating now."

"Napkin also said that I get to mate him first, before any other women. Before *you*."

Eggs grumbled and sneered, but did not argue further. "Fine. I can wait." Then she leaned in close to Pickle's face and said, "But if you ruin him before I get my chance, I'll mate your brother instead."

She looked at Radishes. The bug-eyed man inched back.

"Every single night," Eggs added.

Then she laughed and hobbled away.

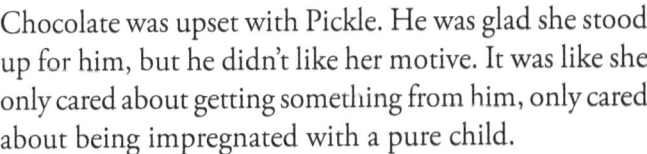

Chocolate was upset with Pickle. He was glad she stood up for him, but he didn't like her motive. It was like she only cared about getting something from him, only cared about being impregnated with a pure child.

Radishes could tell what Chocolate was thinking and told him, "Don't worry, Pickle doesn't actually plan to mate you. She just said that to put Eggs in her place."

Chocolate looked at Pickle. The froglike girl walked ahead of them, leading the way through the underground shanty town, pushing back the mutants that wanted to get a piece of the newcomer.

"Pickle has tried to have children before," Radishes continued. "Four times. But none of them survived. Three miscarried. One was stillborn. She thinks it's impossible to have children now. She said she would never go through that again."

Chocolate nodded. Looking up at Pickle, he realized that he misjudged her. She was not helping him just so that she could use him for herself. She was just kindhearted. Maybe she was even expressing her motherly side while protecting Chocolate, seeing him more as a child than a potential mate. He almost felt sorry for her.

But when she looked back at him, licking her thin lips with a thin pointed tongue, he wondered if Radishes was wrong about his sister. Perhaps Pickle thought that a pure man like Chocolate was a new hope for having a child that could survive her freakish womb.

"Eggs said that she would mate with you if Pickle

ruined me," Chocolate said to Radishes. "What did she mean by *ruin?*"

Radishes nodded. "It's a recent problem in Subway. There's a disease that some women carry that can infect the men they mate."

"What kind of disease?"

"It causes men to be unable to seed. Their mating organ becomes soggy."

"You mean impotent? They can't get an erection?"

"Yeah, but they also become soggy. It turns their organ into goo, kind of like tapioca pudding. They usually fall off when mated."

Chocolate's eyes bulge open. "What? How many women carry this disease?"

"About half of them. Maybe more."

"And it's still a rule that they can mate with any man they want? Shouldn't it be against the rules for them to spread their disease?"

Radishes shrugged. "They probably wouldn't have made the rule if they knew about the disease, but it didn't start happening until generations after the rule was in place. Once a rule is in place it never changes."

"But how can that be good for the future of the species if men's dicks are falling off?"

Radishes didn't have an answer to that. "Not all men succumb to the disease, even when mated by a carrier. It might just infect the men of poor stock."

Chocolate shook his head. He couldn't believe he was stuck in such a society. The idea of being forced to mate with these freaks was horrifying enough. Now he was likely to lose his penis in the process, especially with him being the most pure, and therefore most desirable, breeding male in town.

"We need to get you a guide so that you can go to Store," Pickle told Chocolate once they returned to their shack. "You can stay in our home for now, but you will need to get your own food."

Chocolate nodded. He completely agreed. He wanted more than anything to go to the grocery store. Not just to get food, but because he wanted to see the woman in the blue dress again.

"You should go to Store tonight, if possible," Pickle said, sitting down on the couch and leaning back to rest her wiry flesh. "But you'll need to find a guide to go with you."

"Won't you guide me?"

Pickle shook her head. "We won't be going with you. We have enough supplies to last us for a few weeks, so we won't go back there any time soon. Besides, we are not guides. Guides are the ones who teach young people how to survive in Store. They know more about Store than anyone in Subway and go there several times a week rather than just once or twice a month. You have to give them half of your groceries in exchange for their services, but it's worth the price. You wouldn't survive otherwise."

"Which guide would take me?"

Pickle thought about it, squinting her frog eyes at

the fire pit by her feet.

"Eggs is a guide," she said. "But you don't want to go with her. She takes advantage of her pupils, usually asking for more than half of their groceries. With you, she would likely want even more than that, and I'm not talking about extra cans of soup. In addition to that, her pupils have a very low survival rate. Only one in three ever make it back. She is by far the worst guide in Subway."

Chocolate nodded. She didn't have to explain why Eggs was the wrong guide to take him.

"Who is the best guide in Subway?" Chocolate asked.

Pickle didn't have to think about it. "Milk is by far the best. She knows more than anyone about Store. But I think you should go with someone like Bologna or Plastic Forks. Or maybe Speed Stick—he's a newer one, but not a single pupil has ever died with him."

"Why not Milk? If she's the best I want to go with her."

Pickle hesitated to explain. "Forget about Milk. I shouldn't have brought her up."

"What's wrong with her?"

"Well, she's not a very nice person. She's almost as bad as Eggs."

"But she's good at being a guide?"

"She's the daughter of Cocoa, the only man to survive the Vortex. So, yeah. She was trained by him and knows just about everything there is to know about surviving Store. But *everyone* wants to go with Milk, so there's usually a long wait to go with her. Not only that, but she's really strict. She won't let anyone go with her unless they memorize all the patterns. You really should choose a different guide."

"What do you mean by *memorize the patterns?*"

"Store's patterns," Pickle said. "The ghosts of Store all do the exact same things every night. They move in a pattern. If you pay attention to the ghost shoppers, know where they are and when, then you won't lose track of time or get lost in the Vortex. It's very effective, but very few people are ever able to memorize all the patterns like she can. You'll train with her for weeks and then she'll refuse to take you at the last minute, just because you forgot one little thing about one shopper's pattern. But those who train with her become so good at surviving in Store that they often become guides themselves. Speed Stick was one of her students. He's probably just as good as her but isn't as strict or mean."

"So I should go with Speed Stick?" Chocolate asked.

Pickle nodded. "He's your best option."

But Speed Stick was not a possibility for Chocolate. When Pickle took him to meet the guide, he refused to even consider him. He already had way too many pupils to deal with. His reputation as the best new guide had spread throughout Subway. All of the young mutants wanted to train with him.

So they tried the second best option, Plastic Spoons, who was the guide who trained Radishes when he was young. But she said she was retired. She had enough food and supplies from all her years of being a guide, she no longer needs to go to Store for the rest of her life. And since she was an old lady at almost twenty-eight years of age, she knew her life wasn't going to last much longer.

They couldn't go with Bologna, either. He was one of the strongest, fastest, and smartest guides. He even trained under Milk's father when he was young. But unbeknownst to Pickle, Bologna had gone missing for the past few weeks. They say he disappeared into the Vortex with his last pupil. Nobody had seen him since.

After it was clear that all of the top guides were no longer options, Chocolate and Pickle went looking for the lesser guides. But even these guides all refused. They wouldn't explain why. They just refused to take him.

Exhausted, the two wastelanders sat down at a grease-caked table in one of the communal eating areas. The place reminded Chocolate of the cafeteria he'd eaten at back in the bunker, only this place didn't have a kitchen or serve any food. It was an area where people would bring their own meals in order to eat publicly, with friends and neighbors. Mutant families gathered at tables around them, eating baked beans out of steaming hot cans.

"Something's not right here," Pickle said, wondering what was going on with all the guides they'd spoken to.

"Why are they refusing to take me?" Chocolate asked. "Is it because I'm an outsider?"

Pickle shook her head. "No, even the most desperate guides are refusing. They wouldn't care if you were an outsider or not. There's something else going on here…"

She thought about it for a minute. There was only

one reason she could come up with.

"Eggs…" Pickle said. "It had to be her."

"What do you mean?"

"She probably found out that you're looking for a guide, so she told all the others to back off so that you'd have no choice but to go to her."

"Can she do that?"

"She can intimidate pretty much anyone into doing what she wants," Pickle said. "Nobody wants to cross Eggs, especially not any of the male guides."

"Then what am I going to do?"

Pickle thought about it. Then frowned. "There's only one guide who isn't scared of Eggs, but we already ruled her out."

"Who? Milk?"

Pickle nodded. "Yeah, we have to ask her. She probably won't take you, but it's worth a shot."

CHAPTER FOUR
MILK

Milk lived far away from the other mutants. Her home was deep within an abandoned tunnel, a place littered with ancient bones and rusted train cars.

"She probably won't like you," Pickle said, leading Chocolate down the whispery tracks. "She really doesn't like anyone."

They come to an old car, the only one that hadn't been completely stripped of parts generations ago. There was a light flickering inside, but the car was silent. Plastic shopping bags were taped to the windows so that nobody could see within.

Pickle knocked on the door. "Milk? Are you home?"

The whole car shook as a figure inside stood up out of bed.

A woman's voice: "What do you want?"

"It's me. Pickle."

"Who?" the voice asked.

"Pickle. You know. We used to play together when we were kids."

"I don't care who you are. What do you want?"

"I'm with somebody who needs a guide," Pickle said to the door.

"Go away. I don't need any more pupils."

"This one's special," Pickle said.

"Special how?"

"He's not from Subway. He came from far away."

"That's impossible."

"It's true. Just look at him. He doesn't know anything about Store, so he needs a good guide. You have to take him."

The door opened. A skinny woman with ratty hair stepped out. She wore pants and a tank top she made herself out of black garbage bags. Her skin filthy with ash and grease. Chicken bones and beer caps were woven into her long dreadlocked hair.

"Let me have a look at him." Milk went to Chocolate and grabbed his chin, squeezing it tightly with long black fingernails, examining his face and skin. She was so close that Chocolate could see the grit in her teeth. "He doesn't have any mutations?"

Pickle nodded. "He grew up in a bunker. His people didn't have any mutations. Their genes are even purer than Station's were."

As Milk examined him, lifting his sleeves and peeking down the collar of his shirt, she nodded in approval. It was like she was appraising him, like he was some kind of product on the market.

"I'll take him," she said.

"You'll be his guide?" Pickle asked.

"If he's suitable," Milk said, "I'll give him a shot."

Pickle smiled and patted Chocolate on the back, but he didn't seem too thrilled about the idea. Milk was the scariest of the mutants he'd seen, even though she wasn't the most hideously deformed. If Pickle was froglike, Milk could be described as ratlike. Her eyes were black and beady. Her nose and mouth outstretched, almost like she had a muzzle. But the creepiest part of her were the long rodent tail-shaped growths that dangled out of her hair. There were five of them, like dreadlocks made of flesh.

"Come on," Milk said to Chocolate, tilting sideways to let him inside.

She smelled of skunk and hazelnut as he squeezed past her into the train car.

Before Pickle could come in behind him, Milk held out her bony fingers and said, "Not you."

Pickle's mouth drooped open. "But…"

"I don't need you," Milk said.

Then she shut the door in Pickle's face.

Chocolate didn't feel comfortable being separated from Pickle, especially not when left with somebody as intimidating as Milk. She seemed different than the other mutants in Subway. More animalistic. More feral.

Scanning the subway car, it wasn't a bad dwelling compared to the place Pickle and Radishes lived in. The walls and floor were filthy and the place was a bit cold, but it was spacious. One side of the car was all shelves filled with thousands of items collected from the

Super Foods. A large section contained canned goods and bottled water, but she also had plenty of tools and equipment. A lifetime supply of garbage bags, paper plates, plastic utensils, toiletries—not that she used them—and magazines.

"Seed me," Milk said.

When Chocolate turned around, he saw her removing her plastic clothes. He leapt back at the sight of her naked body, crashing over a makeshift coffee table onto a row of subway seats she used as a couch.

"What?" Chocolate cried, blocking her with his hands. "No…"

Her expression became annoyed. "What do you mean *no?*"

Despite Chocolate's resistance, Milk didn't stop taking off her clothes. Her body was even creepier when naked. The nipples and areolas on her pointed breasts were wide and black as licorice, even though her skin was as white as paper. From her backside grew a long fleshy tail that wagged slowly and curled around her leg like a snake. Milk really was like a rat in more ways than Chocolate cared to know.

Chocolate argued, "Your leader, Napkin, said that because I'm not from your society I don't have to agree to mate with anyone if I don't want to."

"So?" Milk said, shrugging her bony shoulders as she tossed her clothes onto the floor. "I don't have to agree to be your guide if I don't want to."

Chocolate shook his head. "I'm not going to agree to that. If you won't be my guide then I'll just go by myself."

"Then you'll die. It'll be a waste."

"I don't care."

Milk stepped forward. She was not in the least bit awkward with her clothes off.

"Look," she said. "I've been wanting to have children for a long time now, but none of the men down here are good enough. They aren't breeding material. The purest male in Subway won't be of mating age for another five years, and I'll probably be too old to have kids by then."

"I'm sorry, but I was raised differently from your people," Chocolate said, inching away from her. "We don't go around mating with each other just because someone wants to."

"You don't have any food, do you?" Milk asked.

Chocolate shook his head.

"Then you need to go to Store soon, or you'll starve," Milk said. "It normally takes me weeks to train a new pupil, but because you don't have parents providing for you like the rest of my pupils, you'll have to be trained within a day or two. That's asking a lot of me. Extra groceries isn't worth the effort. Seed me and you have a deal."

Chocolate looked into her beady black eyes. "You can really teach me in a day or two?"

"Not adequately," she said. "But enough so that you'll be able to survive one trip. You'll at least do better than you would with any other guide you could find."

Milk didn't wait for him to give her an answer. She scuttled on top of him like a crab and kissed his ashy neck, her tail wagging against his thigh. Chocolate didn't say or do anything as Milk groped him, his eyes wide open, his muscles tensed up.

Not responding to Milk's advances frustrated her.

"Take off your clothes," Milk said.

He did nothing, his facial expression frozen in shock. She put her bony fingers down his pants and grabbed his penis. It was flaccid. After two minutes of trying to make him erect, she groaned in his face and stepped off him.

"Fine." She took an empty tin can from her shelf and placed it on the table next to him. "Just put it in a cup then, you little pussy."

Then she grabbed her clothes and stepped out of the room, leaving him alone to jerk off into the tin container.

"You'll have to stay here for the next couple of days," Milk said.

She sat across from Chocolate, still naked from the waist down, injecting his sperm into her with an eye dropper as she spoke to him.

"We'll sleep at the same time, eat at the same time, shit at the same time, and all the rest of our time will be spent preparing for your trip."

Chocolate couldn't look at her as she applied his seed to her womb, doing it as casually as applying polish to her toenails.

"The most important thing you have to remember is to do what I say at all times," she continued. "Don't ask questions. Do as you're told. Follow my every step.

In Store, you must become my shadow. Move as I do, think as I do."

Chocolate nodded.

"This is the most important thing for you to master," she said. "For the next two days, you must follow this dynamic. I want you to move as I move, copy my every step, no matter what I'm doing."

Chocolate nodded.

"Start now," Milk said. "Shadow me."

Chocolate just sat there, looking at her as she sat in the train seat with her legs spread, the ear dropper in her hand.

"You're already failing," Milk said.

"You want me to… what?" Chocolate asked.

"I told you not to ask questions. Do everything I do, no matter how trivial or ridiculous you think it might be."

Chocolate didn't think she could possibly want him to mimic what she was doing, but he did it anyway. He stepped over to her, sat behind her, and spread his legs in the same manner, copying her motions.

Milk watched him follow her movements through a mirror on the wall across from them.

"Good," she said, as Chocolate imitated her squirting motions. "Practice shadowing me every chance you get, no matter what I'm doing. Shadow me while I'm eating, sleeping, taking a shit. I don't care. You won't be able to memorize the patterns in time, so this will be your best shot for survival. Just make sure not to separate from me."

When Milk was finished, she lifted her knees to her shoulders and leaned her body all the way back, flexing her vaginal muscles to keep as much of the sperm inside of her as possible. Chocolate tried to imitate her maneuver, but he couldn't lift his knees that high. He also couldn't keep a straight face as he curled himself into a ball. She didn't scold him for doing it wrong. The fact that he was attempting to shadow her silly-looking movements without needing to be told was all she wanted of him at that moment.

"The next important thing for you to learn are which products to go for," Milk said. "You'll want to know what foods are perishable, what foods are healthiest, what foods need to be cooked, the different uses for the different items, and what items are valuable in the community and good for trade."

"I already know most of that stuff," Chocolate said. "Even the things I've never eaten or used before, I've seen them in movies. I don't know their value here, but I know about pretty much everything that is sold in the store."

Milk didn't seem to know what he meant by movies, but she didn't ask him to find out. "Good. Before you go, you should decide which groceries you want ahead of time and make a mental map of how to get everything you want in the most direct route possible. By doing this, you will be able to collect more groceries in a shorter span of time. Because you'll be going with me, I will choose the route for you the first time. The next time we go, you will choose your own route if it meets my approval."

Chocolate agreed.

As Milk rocked her weight back and forth, she let out a loud fart. Chocolate tried to imitate her, but when he couldn't let out a real fart he just made the sound with his mouth. Milk was not amused by the impersonation in the slightest.

For the rest of the day, Chocolate shadowed Milk. They raced shopping carts through the abandoned tunnels of Subway. Milk led the way, turning and stopping, placing rocks and old cans into her cart, then speeding away. Chocolate did everything he could to keep up with her. Milk did everything she could to lose him. But, by the end of the practice session, Chocolate did rather well for his first time, compared to most of her past pupils. Though, to be fair, Chocolate was almost twice the age of a typical pupil.

There was a map of Store inked on the side of an old train car in the heart of Subway. It was a large diagram that detailed all the locations within Super Foods. It showed the entrances, the cash registers, the bakery, the deli, the produce section, and even the back store rooms and offices. A list of foods was written in each of the aisles.

Milk placed a collection of different colored magnets on the map, which adhered to the sheet of metal the illustration was drawn upon. Each magnet represented a different shopper.

"This is how Store is laid out when the haunting begins," Milk said. "Try to remember the patterns."

The ghost shoppers each had a nickname the mutants had been using for generations. They called the bearded man, represented by the red magnet, Mr. Fuzzy. The old couple were Mr. and Mrs. Raisin, with dark and light gray magnets. The mother and her children were Mrs. Hen and her chicks, represented by one large yellow magnet and two small yellow magnets. The three teenagers were pink magnets, known as the Giggling Girls. And, of course, Chocolate knew exactly who the blue magnet represented. It was the woman in the blue dress, who they called Miss Blue.

There were several other shoppers Chocolate hadn't seen yet, the ones who were on the other side of the store during his brief visit.

They included:

Mr. Wheels—a morbidly obese man in a mobility scooter.

Mr. Tuxedo—a groomsman on his way to a wedding ceremony.

Mr. and Mrs. Black Eyes—a couple who wore matching sunglasses and leather jackets.

Mrs. Flowers—a woman with flowers on her dress.

Four cashiers—Blond Cashier, Bald Cashier, Mustache Cashier, and Foxy Cashier.

Six other employees—Manager, Meat Man, Mrs. Breads, Security Man, Broom Lady and Smoke Break.

Mrs. Witch—some girl in black clothes and makeup.

Mr. Beers—a guy in a baseball cap buying enough beer for a whole party.

Mr. Turtle—Milk didn't know how else to describe him other than that he was supposed to look kind of like a turtle.

All of these people were the victims of the massacre that took place in Super Foods before the Great Disaster. Chocolate had to repeat their names over and over again, trying to remember all of them and their positions.

She moved each magnet to illustrate their locations for every minute of the haunting. Chocolate couldn't believe she had all of this memorized. The event that repeated at the Super Foods had been permanently stained on her mind since she was very young.

"He's the most important to focus on," Milk said, pointing at the red magnet. "When Mr. Fuzzy is at the end of the soup aisle, that's when you need to leave."

Then Milk placed several steel-colored magnets against the map. "These are the Eight Devils. You want to be out of Store before they appear. Although they cannot see or hear you, their bullets will still hit you. This is the most common way that our people die in Store. They get caught in the crossfire, because they don't know the patterns like I do."

"You know how to avoid the bullets?"

Milk nodded. "If I was stupid enough to stay in Store after the Eight Devils arrived, yes. I know every shot fired and where to stand to avoid being hit. My father forced me to go through it many times."

"He did what?" Chocolate asked. "He made you dodge bullets, just to train you?"

"I watched him do it so many times that it was easy by the time it was my turn," Milk said. "I don't make any of my pupils do this, however. I teach them to play it safe. I teach them to never stay in store for longer than necessary. But my father wanted me to know everything about Store. He wanted me to be able to survive no matter the situation, even if I got stuck in the Vortex."

Chocolate nodded.

"He also wanted his knowledge to be passed down to future generations." Milk turned to him. "That's why I want to have a child so badly. I need to pass his knowledge down to my young. But it can't just be any child. It must be as healthy and pure as possible. It can't have any weaknesses."

"You were raised by your father?" Chocolate asked. When Milk nodded, he asked, "I thought your people were only raised by your mothers, because couplings are outlawed."

Milk shook her head. "Couplings aren't outlawed. Just exclusive mating rights between couplings are not permitted. Men and women are still allowed to fall in love. They are still allowed to raise children together. It just isn't very common, because most women mate with whoever they want, whenever they want. Many of them don't even know who the fathers of their children actually are."

"But your parents were different?"

Milk shrugged. "That's what my dad told me. But they didn't raise me together. My mother died in childbirth when I was born. I never knew her. My father raised me."

"That's kind of sad…" Chocolate looked away from her, looking at the rubble beneath his feet.

"What about you?" she asked. "Were you raised by your parents?"

"Yeah, but they hated each other. Most parents hated each other where I'm from. It's because they were forced to live together and raise children even if they didn't like each other or have anything in common. My parents preferred focusing on their work than spend time with each other, or me…"

When a sad expression crossed Chocolate's face, Milk changed the subject.

"We're getting off topic," she said. "Let's get back to training. You don't want to die on your first trip to Store, do you?"

Chocolate shook his head.

Milk pointed at the magnets, showing him the positions of all the shooters as they entered the store. "Then pay attention."

Then they got back to work.

CHAPTER FIVE
EGGS

The more time Chocolate spent with Milk, the more comfortable he became around her. She was still strange and intimidating, but she wasn't as creepy. For some reason, she seemed more human than the rest of the mutants in Subway, even though she had a tail and looked kind of like a rat.

He had to share a bed with her that night. Besides the smell that reminded him of sleeping in a rat's nest, he didn't mind it that much. It was much more comfortable than Pickle's couch. And because they slept more than ten inches apart, with separate blankets, it didn't really feel like he was sleeping with anyone else.

But Milk seemed to enjoy having Chocolate in the bed with her. She said that her father used to share that bed with her when she was a little girl. She said she missed having that warmth radiating through the mattress. Chocolate had never seen anyone sleep so soundly as Milk did that night.

The next day, they went to the meeting hall. Everyone going to Store each night would gather in the meeting hall earlier in the day, to see who else would be going there that night. It was one of the rules of Subway. Some people liked to work together as a team. Others wanted to make sure everyone stayed out of their way.

"How many people typically go to the store each night?" Chocolate asked Milk as they walked to the meeting hall.

"It varies," she said. "Some days, there will be dozens of people going. Other days, you'll be the only one."

"Which is better?"

"I think it's better to go alone, so that nobody gets in my way. Most people like going in a large group. It makes them feel safer. But you can't move very quickly with too many people. They tend to block the aisles with their carts while collecting groceries. Escaping can also be difficult if too many people are trying to leave at the same time."

"Do you usually go when nobody else goes?"

Milk shook her head. "Sometimes, but it's difficult to predict. Everyone who wants to go alone tries to predict when nobody else is going, but then they end up all going together. And dealing with a bunch of loners who refuse to work as a team is the worst case scenario."

"So you hope we'll be the only ones going tonight?"

Milk nodded. "Yeah, alone with your guide is always better when in training. The only downside to going alone is that if you die while in Store, nobody will know what happened to you. Your neighbors eventually realize you've been missing for a while and assume the worst."

When they get to the meeting hall—which looked a bit like a small underground church constructed on the subway platform, right below the escalators—they immediately realize that they wouldn't be going to the grocery store alone that night. Several people were gathered in the seats, talking to each other. Milk and Chocolate hoped they were the last two to arrive that day. More than this amount and it wouldn't be good for anyone.

The first face Chocolate saw was one he recognized. Her bulbous smile stretched across her face, relishing Chocolate's look of shock when they made eye contact.

"Aw, shit…" Milk said, shaking her head in revulsion. "Eggs is going tonight…"

She said it out loud so that everyone in the meeting hall could hear, including Eggs. Even Milk didn't like the repugnant woman.

"Nice to see you, too, Milk," Eggs said, her smile turning to a grimace.

Chocolate assumed Eggs wasn't there by chance. She'd come for a reason. She knew Chocolate and Milk would be going out that day and wanted to be sure to go with them. He had no idea what she had planned. Sabotage his relationship with Milk as his guide? Make sure he survived so that she'd be able to mate him in the near future? Or maybe just because she wanted to harass

Milk, because that rat woman had something she wanted.

"I see you're still pretending to be a guide," Milk said to her, nodding toward the people gathered around the monstrous woman.

There were three of them with Eggs, all around the age of thirteen—the age children typically became adults and had to support themselves. All of the children were hideously deformed and none of them seemed to be all that bright. A lumpy chubby-faced blond girl, a scrawny little boy with tiny eyes and lizard-like skin, and a tall boy with half of his face melted off—Chocolate wasn't sure if he was in some kind of horrible accident or if he was born that way. Because she was the worst guide in Subway, Eggs' pupils were also of poor quality. They were probably too dumb and unfit for any of the other guides to waste their time with them.

"Are these all your pupils?" Milk asked her.

Eggs nodded. "Yeah, the three who will be going tonight." She introduced the lizard-skinned boy. "That's Stickers." Then she pointed at the chunky-headed girl. "Butter." And finally, the melted-face boy. "Ham Salad."

"You're seriously going to take all of them with you tonight?" Milk asked. "You should only take one pupil at a time. You're going to get them killed."

The already anxious teens became twice as worried by Milk's words.

Eggs rolled her slug eyes. "You teach your kids your way, I'll teach mine my way."

"Your way is why your pupils have such a low survival rate."

Eggs stood up, like she was getting ready to slug Milk with her fat lumpy fist. But she didn't strike, and Milk didn't flinch. The large woman sat back down in her seat.

The six of them weren't the only people going to the Super Foods that night. There was a pregnant woman named Pepsi, who would have been the least deformed mutant Chocolate had seen in the underground if her skin wasn't glowing blue. There was also a man with a distorted face and a long, dangling meaty appendage growing from his chest like a third arm. His name was Budweiser.

"Is this everyone?" Milk asked.

But just as she asked this, two more people entered the meeting hall. Chocolate couldn't believe his eyes when he saw them. It was Pickle and Radishes.

"Here to wish me luck?" Chocolate asked them.

Pickle smiled. "No, we're going with you."

"What do you mean?" Chocolate asked. "I thought you had enough groceries for three weeks?"

"We do." She shrugged. "But we decided to go with you anyway."

Radishes interjected, "*She* decided to go with you. I'm just going for her sake."

"I'm sure you could use the extra help," Pickle added.

Milk got between them and Chocolate. "Actually, we don't need extra help. You'll just be in the way."

Milk glared at Pickle until she inched back. The way she glared at her, it was more than just looking after her pupil's wellbeing. Milk could tell the froglike girl was interested in Chocolate as a mate. She acted as if she were protecting her property.

But even though Pickle was intimidated, she wouldn't back down.

"Well, we're going anyway," Pickle said. "We just want to make sure he's safe. We'll stay out of your way."

Milk stared her down until she broke eye contact. Then she said, "You better."

Eggs was just as annoyed as Milk by Pickle's presence. She, too, saw Chocolate as her property. She didn't want another competitor messing with her plans.

"If that's everyone, then let's get started," Milk said.

Everyone was in agreement.

Because she was the senior guide and most experienced with Store, Milk took charge of the group. She told them which route she planned to take with Chocolate and told them to stay off of their path. The others all agreed, but Eggs had a problem with everything Milk had to say. Any location Milk said she would be hitting, Eggs said she would be going there at the same time. When Milk changed her route, Eggs changed her route to match. The monstrous woman was purposely trying to be a problem. It frustrated Milk so much that she almost cancelled the trip entirely.

Because Chocolate didn't have anything to do with the decision-making process, he sat off to the side next to the pregnant woman with the glowing blue skin. She sat quietly, cradling her stomach. It looked like her baby was due any day now.

"You're about to go to the store in your condition?" Chocolate asked. "Isn't it dangerous?"

The woman smiled. She was one of the more bashful mutants Chocolate had met, unless she was just acting bashful around him.

"Of course," she said. "But it's always dangerous going to Store."

"But isn't it more dangerous when you're pregnant?" he asked.

She rubbed her swollen stomach. "It just means that I won't be able to get as many groceries per visit and I have to make sure to leave early so that I won't ever have to make a running escape. The only real danger is going into labor while I'm there."

"You don't have anyone to go to the store for you?" he asked.

She shook her head.

"I'm taking my last trip before the baby is born," she said. "I won't be going out for several weeks after that."

"Do you have enough groceries to last you?"

She nodded. "Actually, I've been saving up extra supplies for months. The main reason I'm going tonight is for the naming ceremony."

"What's the naming ceremony?"

"You don't have a naming ceremony where you're from?"

Chocolate shook his head.

"What's your name?"

"It was Chocky before I came here, but Napkin changed it to Chocolate because she didn't think my real name made any sense."

The woman smiled. "Chocolate is a good name. I always liked that one. My name is Pepsi."

"Are you all named after groceries?" Chocolate asked.

She nodded. "A mother names her child by taking an item from Store and presenting it to our leader. My mother took a two-liter bottle of Pepsi Cola, and so I was named Pepsi."

"What are you going to name your child?" Chocolate asked.

"I'm not sure. It depends on what I find. A lot of people want to name their children after deli foods, because they are the hardest to get to in time. Pastrami, Prosciutto, Muenster Cheese, Mozzarella Balls, Ambrosia Salad. Those names are all sought after because of how rare they are. But I don't care if my baby has a rare name. I'm more interested in a sweet name. Like Cupcake, Gummy Worms, Starburst, Honey, or even Chocolate, like you."

"So you're going to go right to the candy section?"

Pepsi nodded excitedly. "I'll probably just grab one of everything from that aisle and then decide once I get home. That's not really how it's supposed to be done. You're supposed to go with the first thing you find, typically at random, but nobody ever does that anymore."

Chocolate folded his hands in his lap. The names of the mutants in Subway made more sense to him after his conversation with Pepsi. He understood why Napkin changed his name to Chocolate. It was a much better way to name a child than his people's method. In the bunker, they just used a random word generator on the computer. Whatever it came up with was your name. Most of the names were nonsensical. Chocolate was lucky to get Chocky when he was born—at least it was pronounceable. Some kids were stuck with names like Tyajikwha or Jukakique. The woman Chocolate was matched with, the one who would have been the mother of his children if the bunker wasn't destroyed, was given the name Lunchkin. It wasn't the worst name given to a girl in the bunker, but Chocolate found it rather unappealing for some reason. It sounded like the name someone from the old world would give to a plump pet guinea pig.

After the meeting wrapped up, it didn't seem like an arrangement had ever been made between Milk and Eggs. Milk just gave up arguing and told her to go mate herself, then she grabbed Chocolate by the arm and pulled him out of there. On the way out, he waved goodbye to Pickle and Radishes.

Pickle yelled, "See you tonight."

But Chocolate didn't get to say anything back before he was taken away.

Walking back home, Milk said, "That bitch is going to be trouble."

"Eggs?"

Milk nodded. "She's going to get everyone killed. Napkin should have banished her years ago."

"What should we do about her?"

"Just ignore her. Don't let her distract you. If she gets in our way I'll knock her on her ass."

"Wouldn't it be better not to antagonize her?"

Milk shook her head. "There's nothing we can do that won't antagonize her. We should tie her up in the back of Store and let the Vortex take her."

Chocolate looked at his guide as she kicked bits up rubble out of her path. She was probably just saying it out of anger, but he thought maybe she was serious. Maybe Milk really did want to get Eggs killed. She was a rather frightening woman.

In the final hours before their departure, Milk put her student through as many drills as she could fit in with the short amount of time they had, training him to shadow her and trying to get him to memorize as much of the patterns as possible. But there was only one pattern Chocolate was able to focus on. It was Miss Blue's pattern. He remembered all of her positions in the grocery store, knew her entire path by heart. All he cared about was seeing her again. She was more important to him than Milk, Pickle, or any of the mutants living in Subway.

When it was time to go, Chocolate shadowed Milk as they put on their clothes, strapping garbage bag hoods over their heads, goggles over their eyes, and makeshift filters over their mouths—constructed with aluminum cans and fabric softener sheets.

"You ready?" Milk asked, as they examined themselves

in her bedroom mirror.

Chocolate nodded. "Let's go shopping."

They met with the others at the bottom of the escalator. All of them were dressed in protective gear. Chocolate could barely tell them apart. Only Eggs and her massive bulges distinguished her from the rest.

"Don't worry, you'll do fine," one of the mutants said. It sounded like Pickle, but Chocolate didn't recognize her under all the rags and scarves wrapped around her face. She wore a different outfit than the one he saw her in when they first met. "You've already survived Store once. This time it will be a piece of pie."

"Thanks," Chocolate said.

When Milk saw Pickle speaking to him, she got in her face. "I don't want to see you even look at my pupil once we hit the surface."

Pickle whined, "I was just giving him a little support."

"I give him support," Milk said. "I'm his guide. I don't want you messing with our dynamic."

Then Milk took Chocolate up the escalator, away from the frog siblings.

Chocolate could hear Pickle say, "I was just trying to help…" as she was left behind.

They entered an ash storm once they hit the surface, staggering through the hills of wreckage toward Super Foods. There was no light in the sky, yet. It would still be several minutes before the haunting began.

Milk led the way, Chocolate shadowing her close behind. The others were bunched together further behind them, hunched over, fighting the ash storm. Their protective gear wasn't as good as the equipment Milk made. The ash didn't slow her down in the slightest. She was right to go with plastic over cloth.

The light of the Super Foods sign clicked on just as they entered the clearing. They stepped from the ash onto the clean pavement of the store's parking lot. Then cars appeared one at a time, lining the front of the store. Chocolate hadn't noticed the cars the last time he was there. He wondered if they still worked. He wondered if he could drive them through the wasteland, just for the fun of it, even though he had no place to go. But he shook the thought from his head. He had to focus. He had to be Milk's shadow.

The others gathered around Milk and Chocolate, waiting for the store to come to life. It took about ten minutes of waiting before it was ready, before they could go inside.

"Almost time," Milk said.

She raised her hand. Chocolate mimicked her.

When the lights inside the store brightened and all of the food became visible, Milk swiped her arm downward and cried, "Go!"

Then all the mutants ran for the doorway to the Super Foods.

CHAPTER SIX
MISS BLUE

Milk grabbed a shopping cart and gave it to Chocolate, then took one for herself. When Eggs charged into the store, she grabbed Milk's cart and wouldn't let go.

"This one's mine!" she cried, tugging on the cart.

Milk didn't argue with her. She released the cart and grabbed another one, then took off running before Eggs could claim that one, as well.

Chocolate followed her. They skipped the produce section and went across the front of the store, to get away from the other shoppers. Milk knocked over displays of apple sauce boxes and Lays potato chip bags into their carts. Most of the chips missed his cart when Chocolate shadowed her, trying to topple the right side of the display into the basket, littering bags of chips across the tile floor. But Milk was a pro. She knew just how to swipe them into her cart without dropping a single bag. It didn't even take her a full second to fill half her cart.

They raced onward down the aisle. As Eggs raced behind them, the bags of chips got caught in her wheels, slowing her down. When her pupils rammed their carts into her backside, she screamed and hollered at them, pushing poor little Stickers to the floor.

"Don't look back," Milk told Chocolate. "Just ignore them."

They went into a section of the store Chocolate hadn't been to the last time he was there. He didn't recognize the ghosts who were shopping here. He saw two cashiers: a short bald man with tiny round glasses and an attractive woman with a fox tattoo on her arm. They were ringing up groceries for customers who weren't there, ringing up ghosts. Chocolate wondered why those customers were invisible when all the others could be seen. But, after a bit of thought, he figured it out. They were the lucky ones, the ones who got out of the store before the massacre happened. Their ghosts weren't left to haunt the store for all eternity, like the other customers and employees left behind.

Milk quickly dodged the morbidly obese man on his mobility scooter, moving around him with speed and grace, but Chocolate nearly rammed his cart right into him. He missed the man's dangling protuberances by less than an inch.

As Chocolate put item after item into his cart—not even paying attention to what he was getting, just grabbing whatever Milk grabbed—he was introduced to more of the ghosts: the young couple in matching sunglasses and leather jackets, the man in the beer aisle with the baseball cap and sleeveless Warrior's Gym T-shirt, the guy in the tuxedo looking for condoms, the woman in the flowery dress buying a pregnancy test. They all went on shopping, existing in their own ever-repeating world, totally oblivious to all of the mutants racing through the aisles, tracking toxic ash all over the tile floor.

Chocolate didn't care about any of these ghosts. The only one he wanted see was Miss Blue, who was shopping on the other side of the store. Chocolate wished he would just separate from Milk and go find her on his own, but he knew they would run into her eventually, once they got to the produce section.

Pickle kept her distance from Milk and Chocolate, but she kept her eyes on them. She rolled her cart as her brother collected canned foods and beverages.

"Get some soaps," she told her brother. "The perfumed kind."

Her brother didn't argue, grabbing whatever his sister wanted.

Nearby, Eggs scorned her pupils. Completely untrained and unprepared for their visit to the grocery store, the adolescents just ran around grabbing whatever they wanted, breaking open and eating foods they found, unconcerned about saving their supplies for when they got home.

Pepsi was in the candy aisle, deciding on a baby

name. Budweiser was eating ice cream sandwiches in the freezer section, gobbling them down and then squeezing his lumpy forehead once he got brain freeze.

It was a field day for the Subwayans. Chocolate could tell that in the first fifteen minutes in the grocery store, the mutants felt safe and happy. Store wasn't a dangerous place. The massacre had yet to begin. They could enjoy themselves and relish in the bounties Store had to offer.

But Milk did not share in their joys. She was all business. Her father trained her not to get carried away or lose focus. That was how he and his friends got caught in the Vortex, why all the people he cared about died so young—because they were drinking wine, eating Slim Jims, not taking the dangers seriously. He hammered the message into his daughter: Store is not a playground, always be on guard.

Chocolate had no choice but to share her sentiment. If he wanted to do whatever he wanted, it would have to be on another trip, once he no longer needed a guide.

Milk stopped her cart and scanned the store, looking for Mr. Fuzzy. When she spotted him, she glanced back at Chocolate.

"We should go," Milk said. "Now."

Chocolate couldn't believe it was time to go already. He'd been in the store at least twice as long the last time.

He shook his head at his guide. "But we just got here. We still have plenty of time."

"Don't argue," she said. "This is only your first trip. We can come back next week, after you've had more training."

"But nobody else is leaving. I didn't even get any fruit yet."

"You can grab an apple on the way out."

Milk was displeased with Chocolate's backtalk and he knew it, but he didn't care. He wasn't ready to go. He didn't even see Miss Blue yet. There was only one chance he had. When they went through the produce section, he would be able to go to her then.

When the others saw Milk and Chocolate leaving, they followed suit. They knew it was wise to do as the top guide did. Pepsi and Budweiser headed for the exit. Pickle and Radishes gathered the last of their groceries.

But as they raced toward the produce section, Eggs cut them off. Running full speed down the freezer aisle, she rammed her cart into Chocolate's, knocking it over, dumping the contents all over the floor.

"Oops," said Eggs, placing her chubby hand on her cheek. "Guess I wasn't looking where I was going."

Then she laughed and moved on, rolling over his groceries with the wheels of her cart.

"You did that on purpose!" Pickle cried.

As Chocolate lifted up his cart, Milk grabbed him by the arm.

"Leave it," she said. "We don't have time."

"But I'll lose all of my groceries," Chocolate cried. "I'll have nothing."

He wondered if that was Eggs' plan. Maybe she

wanted to prevent him from getting groceries at Store, perhaps so that she could later offer him food in exchange for being seeded. Or perhaps she just did it to get back at him for turning her down.

"You can have half of mine," Milk said. "Then pay me back another time."

But Chocolate didn't listen. He bent down and retrieved his groceries. Pickle and Radishes went to help. They put the items back in his cart one item at a time.

"The devils are going to come," Milk said. "We don't have time for this."

She looked for Mr. Fuzzy. When she recognized his pattern, a look of panic crossed her face.

"Stop," she yelled at Chocolate.

She grabbed him by the hand and gripped it so tightly that the jar of peach jam in his fingers fell to the floor and shattered.

"Let go," Chocolate cried, her nails digging into his skin.

Milk stared him in the eyes and said, "I'm leaving. Shadow me or you will die here."

Then she let go and pushed her cart forward.

Chocolate left the rest of his groceries to Pickle and Radishes, then followed after her.

A rifle blast echoed through the store. The Eight Devils were already inside, killing the cashiers.

Chocolate looked ahead of him into the produce

section. He saw the woman in the blue dress, looking up from the pomegranates, wondering what had made the loud booming noise. She looked just as beautiful as she did the first moment he saw her, with her silky red hair and shiny blue eyes.

He knew he had to do something. He had to save her, take her from her endless nightmare and bring her to safety.

As Chocolate rushed toward the produce section, following closely behind his guide, he saw something in the corner of his eyes. It was the man in the paper bag hood, carrying his shotgun as he walked down the soup aisle. He was the same one who would kill Miss Blue, the one Chocolate had to stop if he wanted to save her.

Without thinking, Chocolate turned the corner and went down the same aisle as the killer.

Behind him, he heard Pickle cry, "Not that way!"

But he kept going. As crazy as it was, Chocolate knew exactly what he was doing.

The killer aimed his shotgun at Mr. Fuzzy—the young man with the well-manicured beard and flannel shirt, who did not notice the man coming toward him. Chocolate raced past Fuzzy, pushing his cart toward the killer at top speed.

Chocolate was completely invisible to the man in the paper bag hood. The killer couldn't see the filthy man rushing at him.

When the cart hit the Devil in the legs, the shotgun fired, missing his target. He fell to the ground. Before the killer could recompose himself, Chocolate pulled the weapon from his hands, pointed it at his face, and pulled the trigger. The paper bag exploded like it was filled with tomato soup, spraying meat confetti across the tile floor. The killer's body went limp.

When Chocolate glanced back at Mr. Fuzzy, he realized the bearded guy was looking right at him.

"What the hell, bro..." Mr. Fuzzy told him. "You just killed that guy."

Pickle and Radishes were at the end of the aisle, staring at Chocolate as he stood there over the Devil's corpse with a shotgun in his hands. Their mouths dangled open in shock.

Milk appeared behind them, peering down the aisle, wondering what was holding up her pupil. Chocolate was surprised she didn't just leave him behind.

"What the hell did you do?" Milk cried, even more surprised than the other Subwayans. She looked like she was ready to kill him.

Chocolate ignored her. His hands were shaking as he retrieved shells from the killer's pockets and put them into his own. He didn't know what he was going to do, but he was determined to see it through. He had to save the woman in the blue dress.

Mr. Fuzzy looked back at Pickle, Milk and Radishes, wondering where the heck they just came from. Then he stepped toward Chocolate and the dead body.

"Dude, that psycho guy was trying to kill me," said Mr. Fuzzy. "You blew his fucking head off." Then he giggled with delight. "That was badass!"

Milk's tone changed from anger to grave concern.

"The patterns…" she said, pointing at Mr. Fuzzy. "The patterns are changing. He should be dead."

She looked back at the two old people behind them, Mr. and Mrs. Raisin. "They should all be dead by now."

Pickle removed her hood and said, "He saved them."

Then she smiled with pointed teeth. When Mr. Fuzzy saw her hideous froglike face, he backed slowly away from her.

The store erupted into gunfire. Everyone ducked as bullets tore through the walls and ceiling above them. The Devils didn't know they were there yet, just shooting randomly into the air to send fear through everyone in the grocery store.

"We need to get out of here," Milk said. "Everything's changed. Anything can happen."

She ditched her groceries and went for the produce section. The others followed her, even Mr. Fuzzy and the old couple.

"Don't worry," Mr. Raisin said to his wife, holding her tightly. "We'll be alright."

When they got to the produce section, machine gun fire sprayed through the blood orange display, splattering red juices everywhere. The group of mutants ducked and hid behind the lemons.

The shooter came into view—a man wearing a plastic grocery bag around his face, tied tightly at the neck. He stepped between the fruits, firing randomly and giggling with delight. Chocolate scanned the area, but couldn't find Miss Blue. She wasn't hiding in the place she was supposed to be.

"What is Crackle Head doing here?" Milk asked when she saw the man with the plastic hood. "He should be on the other side of the store."

Chocolate looked at the exit. Pepsi was outside in the ash storm already, waiting for the rest of the group. Nobody else was out there with her. She was the only one who made it out in time.

"How are we going to get out of here?" Pickle asked. They couldn't go through the produce department. Crackle Head blocked their path.

Milk shook her head. She had no idea. "We don't have time. We're being sucked into the Vortex."

On the other side of the produce department, a familiar figure appeared from his hiding place. Budweiser, the three-armed mutant, made a break for it. While Crackle Head wasn't looking, he ran for the exit.

"He's going to make it," Radishes said.

But before Budweiser could go through the doors, bullets tore through his chest and neck. He fell, dead before he hit the ground. The shooter wasn't Crackle Head. The bullets came from the checkout section.

Pepsi ran deeper into the wasteland as she saw the shooter step toward Budweiser's body. The killer was female, carrying a pink submachine gun. She wore a bright white and pink box on her head—a Hello Kitty box.

When Hello Kitty looked down at Budweiser's body, she didn't seem to know what to make of it. The mutant's corpse was out of place in the Super Foods. The Devil was clearly perplexed by the state of him.

"That's it…" Milk said, shaking her head when she saw the female killer. "We're stuck."

"What do you mean stuck?" Pickle pointed at the windows. "We're not in the Vortex yet. The outside has not changed."

Milk shook her head. "It doesn't matter. Hello Kitty is at the exit. She'll shoot down anyone who tries to escape. Even if we aren't trapped in the Vortex yet, we can't get out now. She won't leave from that spot until everyone inside is dead."

But just as she said that, Hello Kitty walked away. She just left the exit, as though going to tell one of her friends about the strange-looking man she just killed. The patterns had changed, so the Devils' actions were no longer predictable.

Pickle looked at Milk and smiled, "You were saying?"

Milk didn't give her time to gloat. She said, "Let's go," then kept her head down as she went for the exit.

Chocolate didn't follow the others as they went for the exit. He couldn't leave yet. His mission wasn't complete.

Miss Blue was hiding by the bulk food bins this time, instead of the bread section where she normally would be. She still held her shopping basket tightly to her chest, but the killer coming after her wasn't the one with the paper bag hood. Chocolate had already killed that man. It was now Crackle Head who was coming to kill the woman Chocolate loved. And unlike last time, Miss Blue saw him coming for her.

Pickle looked back at Chocolate when he didn't follow after them. She was about to come back and force him to escape with them, but Mr. Fuzzy pushed on the backs of her shoulders, forcing her to go forward to the exit.

Chocolate knew he couldn't waste time. Crackle Head was almost upon Miss Blue. He had only seconds, at most, to stop him.

"Don't!" Blue whined at the killer, holding out her hands, tears rolling from her eyes. "Please, don't…"

Crackle Head giggled, teasing her with his rifle. He didn't fire right away. He just waved the AK in her direction, making airplane noises with the rifle like a mother feeding her baby with a spoon.

"Are we having fun yet?" Crackle Head asked, mimicking a high-pitched cartoon voice.

Chocolate crept around the shelves, trying to get a good shot at the Devil before he was spotted. But all he knew about weapons was what he'd seen in old movies. He didn't know how to aim or hit a target. All he could do was lift it up and pull the trigger. If he was close enough he wouldn't need to have good aim.

Blue whimpered and begged as the shooter stood over her, aiming his rifle in her face like it was his penis. It pleased him to watch her plead for her life before he wiped it out.

"I hope you're having fun." He giggled at her. "I'm having the time of my life!"

He didn't stop giggling until Chocolate jumped out from hiding, standing behind Blue with the shotgun pointed at the Devil's chest.

"Huh?" Crackle Head said, almost amused by Chocolate's surprise appearance, like it was only a friend playing a practical joke on him.

When Chocolate fired, Crackle Head's ribcage exploded and he was thrown backward into the air. His body knocked over the baguette display and landed in the lemons. Yellow citrus rolled everywhere.

Blue looked back at Chocolate, her makeup running down her cheeks. She was shocked to see him standing there with the shotgun. He felt awkward meeting her for the first time in his grubby outfit, wearing garbage bag clothing and covered in toxic ash. But Blue didn't seem to care. She was just grateful to be alive.

"Thank you!" she cried.

She jumped to her feet and lunged at Chocolate, wrapping her arms around him.

"You saved my life…" she said, bawling her eyes out.

Chocolate wasn't sure what to do. He couldn't believe the moment was actually happening. He couldn't believe she was hugging him, thanking him, wanting to be with him, just as he wished she would. After a moment, he decided to just embrace the situation. He wrapped his arms around her, holding her tightly against him, smelling her pretty red hair.

It was all worth it. No matter what happened from there on out, at that moment, Chocolate was happy. If he died, he would do so with no regrets.

When he was finally finished hugging Blue, Chocolate told her, "Come on. Let's get out of here."

She nodded her head, rubbing tears from her eyes. Then she followed Chocolate through the produce section, holding tightly to his arm.

But when he looked out the windows, he saw that the wasteland was no longer there. Outside, he didn't see hills of wreckage and clouds of ash. He saw a blue sky, sunlight, a bustling city. He saw life.

At first, the sunlight made him smile. He had never seen the sun outside of movies. It was something he only dreamed of being able to see with his own eyes. It was more beautiful than he ever could have imagined.

But, when he realized what had happened, his smile fell from his face. With the sun in the sky, that meant he was no longer in his own world. He had been brought into the world of the haunting. He was trapped in the Vortex.

CHAPTER SEVEN
RADISHES

Chocolate wasn't the only one trapped in the Vortex. Milk and the others didn't get out in time, either. When they ran for the exit, the wasteland disappeared right in front of their eyes. The bright sun hanging low in the sky, just before sunset, blinded them, forced them to cower and back away.

They still planned to leave the store. Even if they were stuck in the Vortex, it was safer outside Super Foods than in. But Hello Kitty returned to her post before they could get out, bringing another Devil with her—a man who wore a cardboard television box on his head. The two Devils fired on the group trying to escape, but were so thrown off by their wasteland attire that they didn't get a chance to aim straight before the mutants ran off. Only the old couple, Mr. and Mrs. Raisin, couldn't get away in time.

After Chocolate rescued Blue, he saw Milk and the others running for their lives. The two Devils stayed in front of the exit, firing at them from a distance.

Chocolate ducked, pulling Blue down with him,

before the Devils could see them. He crawled toward Crackle Head's body and took his weapon, then offered it to the woman in the blue dress.

"Know how to use this?" Chocolate asked in a hushed tone, though he wasn't sure if he could be heard over the nearby gunfire.

Blue shook her head.

Chocolate understood. He tucked the assault rifle under his arm, then took extra ammunition clips from Crackle Head's bloody corpse. Although he wanted to catch up to the others, he was worried about Blue. He didn't want to risk bringing the Devils' attention to them. For now, nobody knew where they were. Chocolate wanted to keep it that way.

"Get after them!" somebody yelled, probably Television Face.

Chocolate didn't move from his spot. He heard footsteps rushing through the produce section, following after his friends. Milk and the others jumped the meat counter, rushing into the employees-only section in the back.

The footsteps grew louder as another Devil rushed past Chocolate's position. This man was fatter than the others. He wore a white paper bag on his head, a McDonald's bag, aiming a .45 caliber revolver as he ran. When the plump Devil turned the corner, heading in the direction of the meat department, Chocolate raised the shotgun and fired. The man dropped immediately.

"Follow me," Chocolate told Blue. He took her by the hand and ran for the meat counter. Miss Blue kicked away her high heels along the way.

The second he left cover, Chocolate fired at the two Devils at the entrance. He knew he couldn't hit them, but the gunfire caused them to drop to the ground and get behind cover. They didn't have a chance to fire back at Chocolate before he escaped from the produce section.

After they were in the clear, Chocolate could hear Television Face say, "What the hell was that?"

Neither of the two Devils followed after him.

The McDonald's Devil was still alive, but just barely. He crawled across the floor, leaving a trail of blood behind him. As Chocolate passed him by, he grabbed the man's .45 out of his hands and left him there to bleed to death. He didn't need to kill him. The Devil wasn't going to last much longer.

Chocolate led Blue behind the meat counter and took her into the kitchen, where Milk and the others were hiding. Then he pushed a table in front of the door to keep the Devils out.

The second she saw them, Milk stepped out of her hiding spot, charged right up to Chocolate and punched him in the eye. She didn't care how many guns he was holding.

"Are you fucking kidding me?" she yelled at him.

When Blue saw the emotional state of the ratty woman, she backed away, trying not to get between them.

Milk jabbed her fingernail in her pupil's chest as she scolded him. "You killed a Devil. You fucked up the patterns. What the hell is wrong with you?"

Chocolate smiled. "I killed more than just one Devil, actually."

She punched him again.

"Some of our people died because of you," Milk said. "Their deaths are on your head. *All* of our deaths are on your head."

Chocolate lowered his eyes. He knew she was right, but he didn't mean to get anyone killed. He just wanted to save the woman in the blue dress.

"Taking you on as a pupil was the worst mistake I ever made," she said. "If I'm not even pregnant after all of this, I'm going to strangle you to death."

Pickle came out of hiding. She seemed upset by the words Milk was saying. Not the part about strangling Chocolate. She was upset about the pregnancy. She couldn't believe Chocolate would agree to seed her when he didn't have to.

"We can still make it out of here, can't we?" Pickle asked.

Milk paced back and forth. The sound of shots being fired continued deeper in the store. The Devils still had other shoppers to kill before they'd come for them. They had a small window of time to come up with a plan.

"My father survived the Vortex by hiding," Milk said. "But there's too many of us to hide. And the patterns are all different. I don't know what spots are safe."

"We can't get out?" Radishes asked. "We really have to wait until morning?"

Milk nodded. "We're stuck here."

Mr. Fuzzy stepped forward.

"What about the other exits?" he asked, acting as though he were a part of their group. Chocolate was surprised to see that he was still alive.

"They're guarding the exits," Milk said, humoring the ghost.

"No, the back doors, man," Fuzzy said, waving his arms around wildly as he spoke. "The employee exits."

Milk shook her head. "Those are all blocked."

"What do you mean blocked?" Fuzzy asked.

"The Devils always barricade them. The closest one to us is blocked by a truck. We won't be able to push it out of the way."

"What do you mean by *always?*" he asked.

He went to the closest exit and pushed on the door. It opened only an inch, hitting the bumper of a truck. He pushed on it with all his strength, but it wouldn't budge.

"Shit… She's right." He turned back to the group. "What about the roof? Can we get up there?"

Milk shook her head. "The roof access is on the outside of the building."

"How do you know all of this stuff?" asked Mr. Fuzzy. "Do you work here or something?"

"Because…" Milk rolled her eyes and turned away from him. "Wait, why am I talking to a dead man?"

Mr. Fuzzy was confused by her words. "Dead man?"

Miss Blue was even more perplexed by their situation than the guy with the beard. Ever since she found herself surrounded by the group of grungy mutants, she had been in a state of shock.

When she finally spoke up, her words were frantic.

"What the hell is going on? Who are you people?" She looked at Pickle's bulging eyes, Milk's growths coming out of her hair. "*What* are you people?"

Chocolate tried to calm her down. "It's okay. We're your friends."

"Why do you look like that?" she asked him. "Your clothes."

Chocolate brought her to a chair and sat her down. "It's going to be alright. My name is Chocolate. What's your name?"

"Mindy," she said.

Chocolate knelt down before her, like he was about to propose. He took her by the hand and looked into her eyes. "I'm going to get you out of this, Mindy. Don't worry."

She wiped her tears away, smudging makeup across her cheek. When Chocolate looked back at the others, they were glaring at him, their mouths wide open.

"You can't be serious…" Milk said.

"What?" Chocolate asked.

She pointed at Mindy. "You're going to save Miss Blue? Is that a joke? She's a ghost. You can't save her."

"Don't tell her that," Chocolate said.

Milk marched up to Mindy and poked her in the head. "She's not real. Tomorrow night, she'll be reset and all of this will go back to normal. She won't remember any of it."

Mindy began to cry again. "What's going on? What are you people talking about?"

They ignored her.

"Not necessarily," Chocolate told Milk. "If I save her and get her out of the store she can come home with us."

"No, she won't. She's in a loop. She'll just disappear."

"Has anyone tried before? You take food from the store and it doesn't disappear. Why can't a person be taken as well?"

Milk paused and stared into Chocolate's eyes for a moment. Then she pointed at him. "You planned all this, didn't you?"

Chocolate looked away.

"I'm right, aren't I?" she continued, yelling right in his face. "You came here specifically to try to take Miss Blue out of Store like an ordinary grocery. Do you know how stupid that is?" She backed away. "We're all going to die because you want to seed a ghost…"

"We're not going to die," Chocolate said. "We can fight them."

Milk shook her head. "That's impossible."

Chocolate raised the shotgun and revolver. "We have weapons. We can stop them."

Milk paused, hesitating to go with his plan. None of the mutants of Subway had ever used a gun before. They had never even seen them used in movies like Chocolate had. All they knew about the guns was that they were loud and could kill people.

When Milk finally made a decision, she let out a loud sigh.

"Fine," she said. "Give me the fast gun."

She obviously meant *machine gun* when she said *fast gun*.

Chocolate handed her the assault rifle and gave the .45 to Pickle.

"This better work," Milk said. "There's no way I plan to die in the Vortex."

A voice came over the intercom system.

"Hello, is this on?" said the voice, tapping on the microphone. It sounded like Television Face.

"What is that?" Pickle asked, looking at the ceiling as though it were the voice of God.

Television Face continued, "Hey, Mad Max Wannabe. What the hell do you think you're doing? You're not supposed to kill *us*. We're supposed to kill *you*. Don't you know anything?"

"Who is that?" Pickle asked, confused by the voice in the ceiling.

"The leader of the Eight Devils," Milk told her. "My father said his voice could be heard everywhere in Store if you get trapped in the Vortex. But the words are all different."

Television Face continued, "We're here to kill you. *All* of you. You don't fight back. You run and scream, then bleed and die. Get with the program."

"There are still shoppers hiding around Store," Milk said to the others. "He speaks from the ceiling in order to scare them out of hiding. But now his words are directed at us. He's trying to get us to show ourselves."

Television Face groaned into the microphone.

"Where the hell did you guys even come from, anyway? A Steampunk Convention?" He paused to laugh at his own joke. "You guys are totally ruining our day, do you know that? You especially ruined Rick's day. You blew his ass off. What kind of dirty son of a bitch would blow a man's ass off? That's just cold, Mad Max. You didn't even have the common decency to finish him off. Now he's lying on the floor in here, bleeding all over the place." The voice paused. "Wait… Never mind, I think he just bled out. That's a relief. I was getting sick of hearing his bitching and moaning."

"Where is the intercom system?" Chocolate asked Milk.

She shrugged. She didn't know what he meant.

"Where is Television Face now?" he asked.

He wondered if it was a good time to strike the leader of the Eight Devils, while he was busy speaking on the intercom. If they got rid of him maybe the others would flee.

"Don't bother calling the police," Television Face continued. "Your phones are out of service. So are the police, for that matter. There's really no way out of this. You might as well just come out. If you'd throw out your weapons that would be awfully nice of you."

Chocolate went to the door and peeked through the tiny window at the top. Two more Devils were out there. Both of them had paper bags over their heads like the first Devil he'd killed, only these two wore matching outfits—red and white striped shirts with red hats glued to the tops of their bags.

When Milk looked out there, she said, "The Waldo Twins… They're the worst of them."

They both carried hunting rifles, scanning the aisles for surviving shoppers, trying to find the location of Chocolate and the Subwayans.

"Why are they the worst?" Chocolate asked.

She kept her eyes on the rifles. "When they shoot, they never miss."

They moved away from the window before the Twins could spot them.

Television Face continued speaking over the intercom, "So you want to know why you have to throw your weapons out? Well, because if you don't I'm going to have to kill some of your little friends I have here."

Milk and Chocolate looked at each other. They had no idea who he could be talking about.

"And, boy, they are ugly little things, aren't they?" Television Face said. "Why don't you say something, you little gremlin?"

Another voice came over the intercom. It was a soft, high-pitched voice that was hard to understand due to all the crying between words. "Eggs… I want… to go home… I want home…"

"It's Stickers," Milk said.

The little lizard-skinned mutant had been captured. Then Television Face put on another mutant. It was the lumpy-faced girl, Butter. She didn't say anything. She just cried.

"I'm sorry, but the other freak kid we tried to capture got his face shot off," said Television Face, surely speaking about Ham Salad. "Though, if you ask me, I think I did the ugly fuck a favor."

Eggs must have ditched her three pupils at the first sign of trouble, leaving them at the mercy of the Devils. She probably got out of the store in time, saving herself at the expense of her little subordinates.

"Now, if you don't come out and show yourself, I'm going to kill one of these horrible little freaks," Television Face said. "Then I'm going to kill the other one."

The sound of crying could be heard through the loud system.

"I might just do it anyway," said Television Face. "Just to put the hideous things out of their misery. Where the heck did these kids come from, anyway? A toxic waste dump?"

"What do we do?" Pickle asked. "We can't let them die."

Milk shook her head. "We don't have a choice. There's nothing we can do for them."

Pickle looked at Chocolate, but he just shrugged at her. He didn't have any ties to the mutant kids. He was there to save Mindy and no one else.

"Well, I'm going after them," Pickle said, raising the revolver.

Milk got in her way. "No, you're not."

On the loudspeaker, Television Face said, "I'm going to count to three and if you don't show yourselves, the little girl gets it."

"We have to do something…" Pickle said.

"One…"

Pickle nodded toward her brother and they both tried to move the table from the door.

"You'll get yourself killed," Milk said, pushing the table back. "I won't let you do that."

"Two…"

Pickle struggled against Milk, trying to pull the table. Milk sat down on it, holding it in place with her weight.

"They're just children…" she cried.

"Two and a half…"

Chocolate touched her on the shoulder. "I'm sorry…"

Pickle looked him in the eyes. Tears dribbled down her cheeks.

"Three."

A bullet pierced through the window above Milk's head, cracking the glass, and hitting Pickle in her left eye. Her bulging eyeball popped like a little water balloon and the bullet blew out the back of her head. She went limp, falling into Chocolate's arms.

Radishes screamed. His sister's brains covered his shoulder.

At first, everyone was confused at what had happened. They heard the gunshot over the intercom, but thought it was Stickers who was being shot, not Pickle. Chocolate peeked through the window. It was one of the Waldo Twins, aiming his rifle at them. The second Chocolate and the Devil made eye contact, the Waldo Twin ducked, hiding behind the meat bin. He was different from the other Devils. He played it safe, knowing Chocolate was well-armed.

When Chocolate looked down at Pickle's body, he

realized what a horrible mistake he made. He never should have tried to save Mindy so recklessly. He should have waited until he understood the grocery store better. He should have waited until he had a plan. But, most importantly, hc should've waited until he was alone so that nobody else would have gotten caught in the Vortex with him.

Television Face did a second countdown for the other hostage he had with him. Nobody did anything about it. They just stayed low, away from the window, staring at Pickle's body until the countdown was over.

"Boy, you people are cold," Television said, before he pulled the trigger.

Radishes cried against his sister's cheek, holding her in his arms as tightly as he could. They were even closer than Chocolate realized. She must have been everything to Radishes. His only friend. His only family.

There was no denying it—her death was all Chocolate's fault, and they all knew it. If she didn't like him so much, didn't see him as a potential mate, a little brother, or even a child, she wouldn't have wanted to go to the store with them that day. She wouldn't have gotten sucked into the Vortex.

"We need a plan," Milk said to Chocolate.

He nodded. She took him aside, where the others couldn't hear.

"Any ideas?" she asked.

Chocolate said, "We have to go after them before they come for us, to catch them off guard."

"But they know where we are now," she said. "We won't be able to surprise them. They'll be ready for us."

"We still have the upper hand," Chocolate said.

"How so?"

"They're spread out. They've got two people guarding the exits, right? The leader is in the manager's office, on the intercom system. And the Waldo Twins are just outside. We have five people and three guns. No matter which group we face, we'll always have them outnumbered."

"So you think we should rush them? The Waldo Twins?"

"There's only two of them and five of us. And they can only fire one shot at a time. They couldn't get us all."

"But we only have three guns, so we might as well just be three people. And the Waldo Twins never miss. If we go out there two will die, no matter what. And then the third person will have to try to kill them both before they can get off their next shots. It's not going to work."

"Unless we get them to shoot at something else."

"Like what?" Milk asked.

Chocolate nodded toward Pickle's body.

"You want to use her body as a decoy?"

"Yeah, why not?"

"Don't you have any respect for the dead?"

"Not if it's to protect the living. She's already dead. It doesn't matter."

"You really think her brother would go with that plan?"

Chocolate looked at Radishes. The frog man's eyes were

shut tight, rocking his filthy sister's corpse in his arms.

"He has to," Chocolate said.

"But will it even work? Even if they don't realize Pickle is already dead before they shoot at her, only one of them might fire. The other Twin might go for another target. Whoever goes out second will likely be shot."

"Then I'll go second."

"Are you sure? The Waldo Twins never miss."

"It's my fault all of this happened. I should take the risk."

"You could send Mr. Fuzzy or Miss Blue. They're ghosts. It doesn't matter if they die."

Chocolate shook his head. "No, it should be me. Even if they're ghosts, they don't know it. They're not going to volunteer."

Milk nodded. It was clear she didn't like the idea, but it was the only idea they had.

It didn't take convincing Radishes to use his sister's body. In fact, they didn't even talk to him about it. He was too busy weeping to ask them what they were going to do with her when they took her body away.

Chocolate propped her up against the back of a wheeled chair, holding her up with the back support so that she would stay standing, even if her upper body was slouched to the side.

"What's going on?" Mr. Fuzzy asked. "What are you doing?"

Chocolate pointed at the revolver on the floor. "Do you know how to use that thing?"

Fuzzy shrugged. "I guess…"

"Take it. We're going to make a break for it. If you see one of them, shoot. Don't run. Shoot. It's the only way we'll make it out of this."

The fuzzy man nodded and took the weapon.

Milk went to Radishes and tugged on his arm. "Come on. We're going."

He reluctantly crawled to his feet, but he obviously no longer cared if he lived or died. He wasn't going to be much use to them.

"We can't go," Mindy cried. She was the only one opposed to the plan. "We should stay here until the police arrive. They can't get in. If they try you can just shoot at them."

Milk looked at Chocolate. "She's got a point. If we can wait it out here until morning we'll survive the Vortex."

Chocolate shook his head. "But then we'll be on the defensive. If they come up with a plan of attack before us we'll be at a disadvantage."

"But what if their plan is to wait for us to make the first move?"

Chocolate didn't have a good answer.

He said, "We'll just have to try and see."

Before they could remove the table from the door, they saw smoke pouring into the room.

"What is that?" Mindy cried.

Chocolate quickly peeked out of the window. The whole area behind the counter was on fire. One of the Waldo Twins was throwing bottles of lighter fluid at it, spreading the fire.

"They're trying to burn us out," Mr. Fuzzy said.

"Let's move," Chocolate told them. "Now."

Although the Waldo Twins were expecting them to come out—getting them out was their whole reason for setting the place on fire in the first place—they didn't think the mutants would come out so soon.

Milk and Chocolate pushed Pickle's body through the door, into the flames. A bullet pierced her chest, knocking her sideways. Chocolate couldn't tell where the shooter was coming from, but he saw the Waldo Twin who was starting the fire.

As the Devil raised his arm to throw another bottle of lighter fluid, Chocolate aimed his shotgun at him and fired. It didn't take down the Waldo, but the bottle shattered in his hand, splattering him in the arm and face with flammable liquid that immediately burst into a sheet of flames.

Milk and Chocolate ran forward, leaping over the flaming counter. Mr. Fuzzy came after them, but Mindy and Radishes stayed behind, scared to go through the fire.

As the Waldo thrashed at the fire, the paper bag on his head burning against his face, Milk raised her assault rifle and pulled the trigger. Bullets sprayed everywhere, tearing the devil in half but also shredding nearby groceries on the shelves. When she let go of the trigger, the Devil fell to the ground, fire spreading across his red and white striped shirt.

They killed one of them, but the other Waldo Twin was nowhere in sight.

"Find cover, bro," shouted Mr. Fuzzy, running for the aisles with his revolver pointing the way.

But Chocolate didn't move. He scanned the area, looking for the other Devil. When he finally found him, it was too late. The other Waldo Twin was over a hundred feet away, on top of a freezer shelf. He had Chocolate in his sights, and he was far out of the range of Chocolate's shotgun.

Chocolate thought it was over. All the Waldo had to do was pull the trigger. The Waldo Twins never miss.

When the Waldo Twin fired, Chocolate moved. Just slightly. He shifted his weight a little to the left. And after the shot rang out, Chocolate was still standing.

"He missed..." Chocolate said to himself. "The Waldo Twin missed..."

But then he felt blood dripping down the side of his face. The pain came in a second later. Then his ear fell from his shoulder and landed on his foot.

"Get down, bro!" Mr. Fuzzy cried, too late to do much good.

The Waldo Twin didn't kill Chocolate, but he shot his ear off. Chocolate grabbed the side of his head as blood sprayed down his neck. Then he ran for cover. The Devil didn't have a chance to get off another shot.

Milk, Fuzzy, and Chocolate all knelt behind a shelf in the freezer section, clutching their weapons tightly, watching for Waldo to show his head. When Chocolate looked back at the meat counter, he didn't see Radishes and Mindy. They were still in there and the fire was spreading. He couldn't go back to save them without making himself an easy target. He prayed they could save themselves.

"We can get him," Milk said. "Like you said, he can only shoot one bullet at a time and he can't get all of us."

Mr. Fuzzy said, "Should we rush him?"

Chocolate shook his head. "I've got a better idea."

He ran down the aisle toward Waldo's position, keeping his head down. The others followed. Then Chocolate opened the freezer case and fired into the top of container. He could see Waldo rolling out of the way. Milk and Fuzzy fired through the tops of other freezer cases. As bullets flew beneath his feet, Waldo danced around on top of the cases until he jumped down into the next aisle.

"Let's get him!" Chocolate cried.

He climbed up the freezer case and aimed his shotgun at Waldo's back. Before the Devil could turn around, Chocolate pulled the trigger. But nothing happened. It only clicked. The shotgun was out of shells.

When he heard the clicking noise, the Waldo Twin turned around and aimed his rifle at Chocolate. Then he laughed with relief.

Before the Twin could fire, a shrieking noise threw Waldo off. He turned around. Radishes was racing down the aisle, running straight for him, holding a meat cleaver over his head.

Waldo turned his attention to the mutant. He didn't have time to aim. When he fired, the bullet hit Radishes in the stomach but it wasn't enough to stop him. The Devil didn't have enough time to cock his rifle before the mutant was upon him.

With all of his wrath, Radishes jumped at the Devil and drove the cleaver into his neck. The mutant didn't know if this Waldo was the same one that killed his sister, but he struck him as though he were, chopping him in the face and throat.

Waldo twitched and whimpered as he was attacked. The rifle slipped from his fingers. He tried to crawl away from the madman, but as he turned onto his stomach, Radishes just assaulted his back. By the time the mutant was done with him, the Waldo Twin was covered in gashes, his left arm severed from his body, half his blood splattered across the aisle.

Chocolate was proud of his mutant friend. He wanted to cheer for him, praise him for saving his life. But the second he was finished, Radishes fell to the floor. The mutant collapsed on top of Waldo, his breath slowing to a stop. The bullet in his guts did more damage than Chocolate thought.

When he got down from the freezer case, Radishes was already dead. Chocolate didn't get a chance to thank him for saving his life. He didn't even get a chance to apologize for causing his sister's death.

CHAPTER EIGHT
THE DEVIL

When Chocolate returned to the others, he saw that Mindy was now with them. She escaped the back room with Radishes before the fire could consume the area.

Smoke was filling the grocery store. The fire was spreading. They had to get out of that section of the store before it caught up to them.

"What now?" Milk asked.

"We go for the exit," Chocolate said, reloading his shotgun with shells from his pocket, hoping he was putting them in the right way. "There's only three Devils left and two exits. That means one is guarded by two Devils at most. The other has only one. We go for whichever door has the one."

Milk nodded. "It's probably the west exit. Hello Kitty will be at the east exit and Television Face is more likely to be with her. The west exit is safer."

Chocolate agreed with the plan. Even though the west exit was farther away, it was the best option. They headed in that direction, taking the dead Waldo's rifle and bullets with them.

On their way, they ran into a Devil they weren't expecting. When they saw it, they ducked behind cover.

"Which one is that?" Chocolate asked.

It wasn't Hello Kitty or Television Face. Chocolate looked over at Milk, but she was just as confused as he was.

"I have no idea…"

When they got a closer look, they realized there was something incredibly strange about this Devil. It was fat and deformed, wobbling down the aisle toward nowhere in particular. There was a paper bag over its head, but instead of a weapon in its hands the Devil held a broomstick, pretending the pole of wood was some kind of rifle.

"That's no Devil…" Milk said. "That's…"

"Eggs!" Chocolate cried.

The Devil turned its head and looked at them, pointing the broomstick in their direction. The shopping bag she wore was fresh, like she grabbed it herself from a cashier station and was trying to blend in with the other killers.

"You're still alive?" Milk asked, nearly laughing at her.

Eggs removed the bag from her head and looked at them.

"What the hell are you guys doing out here?" she asked.

She didn't look as terrified as she should have been. Chocolate had no idea how she could have survived so long doing such a poor impression of a Devil.

When Eggs scanned their group, she realized there were some faces missing. She asked, "Where's everyone else?"

"We're all that's left," Milk said.

"Pickle and Radishes?" Eggs asked.

Milk shook her head.

"Come with us," Chocolate said, holding out the Waldo Twin's hunting rifle for her. "We're getting out of here."

Eggs smiled. She didn't hesitate to replace her wooden replica with a real gun. When it was in her arms, Milk looked at Chocolate with an angry face. She couldn't believe he would give the horrible woman a weapon. Before all of this, Eggs would have killed them both given a chance.

When they got to the west exit, they saw only one Devil. He was alone. And he didn't appear to be ready for them. He was hardly standing guard. He just stood there, unarmed. His double-barreled shotgun rested against the door three feet away from him.

"This is too easy," Milk said. "It has to be a trap."

Chocolate nodded. "You stay here, just in case. I'm going to check it out."

"But the others could be nearby," Milk said.

"If they are, you can get the jump on them."

Milk didn't like it, but she let him go.

"Just don't die," Milk said. "You've got a serious beating coming to you once we get out of this."

Chocolate left their hiding spot and snuck around a

candy display toward the Devil. When he showed himself, Chocolate pointed his shotgun at the man guarding the exit. The Devil didn't have a chance to go for his weapon. He didn't even try. He just raised his hands in surrender.

"Don't move," Chocolate said, stepping toward him. "If you go for your gun I'll blow your head off.

"I don't intend to," said the Devil. His voice was different from the others. It was almost friendly. "My gun isn't even loaded."

With those words, Chocolate was confused. It had to be a trap. The Devil had to be lying.

"Where are your friends?" Chocolate asked.

The man shrugged. "On the other side of the store, I guess."

Chocolate kept the shotgun pointed at him. "We outnumber you now. If your friends are trying to set a trap for me, it won't work. My friends will kill them if they try to kill me. And I promise I will shoot you before I die."

"Don't shoot," said the Devil. "I was hoping to get the chance to talk to you."

Chocolate didn't understand what he was getting at.

"I'm going to take my mask off." The Devil raised his hands higher, toward his head. "Don't shoot. I'm not going to try anything."

Chocolate let him. The Devil removed the brown paper grocery bag from his head, revealing his face. He was an older man with a gray beard, small round glasses on his face.

"That's better," the man said. Then he smiled.

He didn't seem at all like what he expected of a Devil. He was just a normal man. He looked kind of like Chocolate's grandfather, the nice one who always gave him treats even when his parents forbade it.

Before he spoke, the two of them had a moment together. The Devil smiled, nodding his head. It was as though he thought Chocolate would recognize him, as though Chocolate would have something to say. But the Devil just nodded, pleased with himself for some reason.

"It worked, didn't it?" the Devil asked.

Chocolate had no idea what he was talking about.

"The plan," the Devil continued. "It worked. You have no idea how relieved I am to know that it worked."

Chocolate couldn't tell if it was still a trap. It was too strange to be. Something was very off about this man.

"What are you talking about?" Chocolate asked.

The Devil smiled again and nodded his head. "You're not from this time, are you? You're not from this world."

Chocolate was taken aback by his words. He lowered his weapon. "What do you mean?"

The Devil explained, "The second I saw your outfits and your friends, I knew you weren't supposed to be here. You're from the future, just as I hoped. That means there actually is a future. You have no idea how happy this makes me. It wasn't all for nothing."

"I'm not following you. You know about the store? You know about how it repeats?"

With those words, the Devil's face lit up. He pumped his fist as though his team just made a touchdown.

"Yes!" The Devil cried. "Oh, thank God, yes…"

He looked like he was about to fall to his knees in relief.

Milk stepped up behind Chocolate. She had been listening to the exchange, just as shocked by his words as her pupil was. Milk and Chocolate looked at each other, then back at the man.

When he saw Milk, he nodded his head at her, almost with pride.

Then he told them a story, "Several years ago, there was a house I heard about. It was an old house. A terrible thing happened there once, a long time before. Something so terrible that it broke time. A family was brutally murdered by their mother. It happened just after ten o'clock, after the children had been put to bed. This thing was so horrendous, so unspeakable, that the souls in the house would not rest. They were doomed to repeat the tragic affair, over and over again, every night, for all eternity."

The man stopped to smile again. He just couldn't keep the smile off his face.

He continued, "For decades, the house was haunted by this event. It reoccurred every night, at the exact same time. The mother would return and murder her family, exactly as she did that first night. There have been other hauntings in the past, other terrible things that have occurred. But this one was special. If you were to enter this house at exactly the time the event took place, you would be brought back to that world. You could sit on the furniture that was used in that time period. You could listen to the gramophone. You could pet the family dog. But the most curious thing about this haunting, which was different from any other haunting that had been documented before, was that you could go into the kitchen and eat their food. You could sit down at the table and drink a glass of wine. You could eat a slice of pie from a recipe that hadn't been used in a hundred years. And not only that, but you could take the food home with you. You could take all their food home with you. And the next day, their cabinets would replenish. Everything would go back to how it was before."

Chocolate and Milk didn't respond to his words. They just listened.

The old man paused, taking a deep breath. He turned away from them, looked out the window toward the sky.

"When we found out that the world was going to end, that the planet was no longer going to be inhabitable for hundreds of years, we had to come up with a plan. We knew there would be survivors. Not everyone would die easily. But how long would they survive? There would be no water left to drink. No food that could be grown. The human race would cease to be. But then we thought back to that house, that place where that terrible thing always happens. We wondered if its cupboards would still be replenished with food every night, even after the world ended. If it did, then somebody could survive off of that food. They wouldn't have to grow anything if there's a never-ending supply to take from."

"So you're saying…" Milk began.

The old man nodded. "We wanted to create a new terrible thing, a new haunted place, but on a much larger scale. It's not just this grocery store. There are groups of killers attacking several stores, all over the city, in multiple cities all over the country."

"So you're all behind this?" Chocolate asked. "All of the Devils killed these people just so they could… save our species?"

The old man snickered a little. "Well, not all of us were in on it. Most of these killers are just ordinary psychopaths, killing these poor people for the sick fun of it. They don't know we're having them do it. They don't even know the world is about to end."

"But if you did multiple mass shootings all over the city, how come there aren't other stores like this one? Outside of this store, there is only wasteland for miles and miles."

The Devil let out a sigh. He paused for a moment, then said, "We didn't know how many massacres would actually cause such a haunting, so we did as many as we could. We hoped some of them, *any* of them, would create the same results as that depraved mother caused in her family home. We knew most would do nothing. But if there was one, just *one*, that worked, it would all be worth it."

"Worth it?" Chocolate cried, thinking about all the innocents that were involved, all of the Miss Blues and Mr. Fuzzies. "You killed so many people…"

The Devil held out his hands. "I know. Believe me, I know. But all of those people would have died soon anyway. It was worth it to save the human race."

"You son of a bitch," Milk said, pointing the assault rifle at him. "Do you know what kind of hell you've put us through? We have to survive this massacre every single night, just to get enough food to eat."

The Devil nodded. "I know. I'm sorry. I can't believe how hard it is for you…"

Milk moved the barrel of her rifle closer to his head. "I ought to kill you for doing this to us."

The Devil did not recoil from the weapon.

"You can kill me if you want," he said. "But because you're here, that means I must have died a long time ago. I'm just a lost soul haunting this place, like the mother who killed her children. The police probably gunned me down before I left the store, many years ago."

Milk pressed the barrel of her rifle right against his forehead, the weapon trembling in her grip.

"You should take as much food as you can carry and go home," said the Devil. "I'm sorry we couldn't have done more for you."

Then he grabbed Milk's weapon and pulled the trigger, blowing his own brains out across the store windows.

CHAPTER NINE
FACE

The fire raged across the grocery store, devouring the breads and produce, burning away the napkins and paper plates, melting all the candies and chocolates.

As Milk stood in front of the exit, waiting for the doors to open, she laughed a crazy rat laugh, breathing in the fire smoke. But something was wrong. The doors weren't opening.

"What's going on?" Chocolate asked.

Milk waved her hands at the door. "They should open on their own. They're automatic."

But the sensor wasn't reading them. The door was closed tight.

The others ran toward them, wondering what was going on.

Milk and Chocolate tried to push the doors apart, but they were stuck. They wouldn't budge.

"It's locked," said Mr. Fuzzy.

Chocolate didn't understand how they could lock. There was no doorknob. No keyhole.

"There's probably a latch on the side or something,"

Fuzzy said, feeling the frame of the door.

They were so close. The exit was just through that glass. But as much as the beardy man tried, he couldn't get it open.

"Stand back," Eggs cried, charging the door with a grocery cart.

Even with all her strength, the cart just bounced off the glass. Milk, Eggs, and Chocolate tried kicking the door, trying to break it off its hinges or shatter the glass. But the material was too strong. Even if they had a sledgehammer, they didn't know if they could get it open.

Chocolate looked back at Mindy. She was giving them room, coughing on the smoke. A look of hopeful desperation was plastered across her face.

"Don't worry," Chocolate told her, going to her and hugging her to his filthy chest. This time, she didn't hug him back.

"I think I found it," said Mr. Fuzzy.

He found something at the bottom of the door, fidgeted with it.

As Chocolate held Mindy, he saw movement over her shoulder. Two figures coming toward them through the smoke.

"Look out!" he cried.

Chocolate pushed the woman to the floor, raised his shotgun and fired just as the Devils came within range. His blast missed, blowing out the back of a self-checkout kiosk. Hello Kitty and Television Face opened fire at the same time, but they weren't aiming for Chocolate. They went for the ones trying to get out the door.

Unlike the Waldo Twins, Hello Kitty and Television

Face weren't good shots. But they didn't need to be. Their bullets tore through the three by the door. Eggs, the largest target, was hit five times in the torso. She fell back, knocking over the cart by the door. Milk was hit twice in the arm, throwing her face-first into the tile floor, dropping the assault rifle from her grip. Mr. Fuzzy was hit with only one stray bullet, but it penetrated his temple, killing him instantly.

Chocolate pumped his shotgun and fired again. It didn't take down either of the Devils, only grazed Television Face's thigh, but the distraction was enough for Milk to get away. She ran for the bathroom, clutching her arm, leaving her assault rifle behind. Before the Devils could turn their attention to Chocolate, he grabbed Mindy and ran deeper into the store, disappearing into the smoke.

They didn't follow after. Before the Devils could fire at Chocolate's fleeing back, a bullet pierced through the pink box on Hello Kitty's face. She staggered back, screaming. Still alive, but dazed by the impact. The Devils couldn't tell where the shot came from until they saw Eggs sitting up from the floor. She was still alive, clutching the hunting rifle in her hands. Even though she was hit five times, her bulbous deformities were cushion enough to protect her vital organs.

"I'll rust your womb, you scrawny slut," Eggs yelled at Hello Kitty, planting another slug in her lower abdomen.

Television Face cried out, rushing for the female Devil. She was obviously someone close to him, a sister or a girlfriend. He was too distracted with emotion to stop Eggs before she cocked her rifle.

Eggs moved her aim toward the male Devil. "I'll melt your dick off!"

Television Face let out a burst of gunfire at the same time Eggs fired her rifle, tearing through her chest.

Eggs was going for the Devil's crotch, but her aim was off, hitting him in the thigh instead. It was still enough for him to cry out in pain, staggering him off balance.

Although she was full of slugs, Eggs still didn't die. She cocked her rifle and aimed it at the Devil's head. "I'll mate your face until you choke!"

But Eggs couldn't get off another shot. Hello Kitty and Television Face both opened fire on her at the same time, splitting her face and ribcage open, emptying the rest of their clips into her. Eggs still survived the blast. She coughed up blood, spitting it at them, still cursing under her breath even with her thick skull broken into pieces.

They put new clips into their submachine guns and pointed them at her.

Eggs died laughing at them.

Hello Kitty removed the pink box from her head, revealing a bloody face. She put her hand to her lips, crying in agony. Eggs' bullet had pierced through her cardboard mask and hit her in the mouth, breaking through her teeth and tongue, exiting through her right cheek.

Television Face removed his mask as well, holding her in his arms, trying to comfort her. When Chocolate saw the Devils' faces, he couldn't believe how young they were. Both of them were just teenagers, younger than Mindy and Mr. Fuzzy, younger than even Milk and Chocolate. He couldn't believe it. Without their masks, they weren't scary anymore. They weren't monsters. They were just scared, troubled kids.

Chocolate thought about going for them at that moment, while they were vulnerable. But he hesitated, missed his chance. He just felt too sorry for them to kill them in such a pathetic state, as they held each other, crying in each other's arms.

But the second Television Face set down his wounded girlfriend and composed himself, Chocolate regretted his decision. The leader of the Eight Devils turned toward Chocolate's position. His face was fuming, filled with wrath for what they'd done to his woman. He pulled his television mask over his head and charged forward. He was ready to destroy anything that got in his way.

Chocolate led Mindy through the smoke, into the freezer section. She coughed and gagged. Chocolate tried to cover her face, keep the smoke from entering her lungs so that she wouldn't make so much noise. But the fire had spread and the smoke was thick and covered everything.

He opened a freezer case and helped Mindy climb inside, folding her blue dress behind her. It would be cold, but safe. The smoke wouldn't get inside. The windows were fogged over from the heat, so she would be practically invisible.

"I'll be back for you," Chocolate said.

She just nodded at him, clutching at the smoke in her neck, as he closed the case and turned his attention to Television Face.

Chocolate pulled his makeshift gasmask over his face and went deeper into the smoke. Unlike Television Face, he'd be able to breathe in the stuff. He'd spent days out in the ash storms, breathing all sorts of gases and toxic grit. This smoke was nothing compared to the atmosphere of the wasteland.

Television Face marched through the aisles, searching for the man responsible for killing so many of his friends.

"It's just you and me now, Mad Max," Television Face called out. "One of us isn't leaving here alive."

Although Chocolate could breathe better than Television Face in the smoke, he couldn't see any better. His goggles prevented his eyes from burning, but they didn't do much to see where he was going. He had to follow the Devil by the sound of his voice.

"I don't really care if I make it out or not, to tell you the truth," the Devil continued, limping down the aisle, tracking blood across the ceramic floor. "In fact, I'm counting on it. There's nothing to go back to."

Chocolate saw his black form coming down the next aisle, but he wasn't within range. He stepped back into the smoke, waiting to get the jump on him.

Television Face coughed and gagged on the smoke, but kept moving.

"The world is about to end," said the Devil, hacking and spitting in his mask.

When Television Face came closer, Chocolate fired.

He shot too soon, too sloppily, still out of range. Shelves of flaming tortilla chips exploded on impact, launching Cool Ranch Doritos into the air.

After the miss, Television Face fired his submachine gun, forcing Chocolate to run for cover.

Once they'd lost each other, Television Face continued, totally ignoring the bullet exchange. "You probably don't know that yet. You probably don't even believe me. But it's true. The world is really going to end. Not today. Not tomorrow. But soon."

The Devil turned the corner, pointing the gun in Chocolate's direction. But Chocolate jumped over a fallen mobility scooter and ran farther into the fire and smoke.

"My father told me this," Television Face continued. "He's a very important man and was one of the first to learn about the disaster that is to come."

Chocolate shot at him again. He couldn't see him through the smoke, he just fired in the direction of his voice. The Devil was unfazed by the attack. He didn't fire back.

"The old man is building an underground bunker not too far from here," Television face said. "Him and his pals in the military. They think they can survive the end of the world. Do you believe that? Instead of enjoying the last days of their lives, they're dumping all their money and resources into one last gamble, trying to buy their way out of the inevitable."

The fire was too high for Chocolate to continue. He couldn't move forward and couldn't go back. He had to take an aisle toward the front of the store, leaving the hidden safety of the smoke.

"The old man wanted me to be a part of it," Television Face continued. "He wanted me to hide down in his tomb and bury myself alive with the rest of them. But that's not for me. Even if they survived the apocalypse, who wants to live in a coffin for the rest of their life?"

When Television Face saw Chocolate exiting the smoke, he fired. Chocolate ran, firing the shotgun behind him as he went.

The Devil kept speaking, "Not me. I'd rather embrace the chaos and die in a blaze of glory."

Chocolate went down the adjacent aisle, firing through the shelves at Television Face. The Devil fired back. Chocolate dropped to the ground and fired low, hoping to hit the kid's legs. None of the blasts connected. The products on the shelves provided adequate shielding.

"How about you?" the Devil asked, after their fire fight halted. "How will you face the end of the world? Will you go out in a blaze of glory, Mad Max?"

Chocolate could hear him grab the shelves, trying to climb up the canned goods rack.

"Nah, I don't think so," said Television Face. "You're the type who fights against his fate. You'll die kicking and screaming, doing everything you can to stay alive right up until the very end."

Chocolate was on the ground, lying on his back. He aimed his shotgun at the top of the shelves, waiting for the Devil to show his face.

"Just like my old man."

When the television box peeked out over the case,

Chocolate fired. The box exploded, blowing shreds of cardboard into the air like confetti. Then the Devil's face appeared, laughing his ass off. The box mask was just a decoy.

Chocolate didn't have time to pump his shotgun. The Devil aimed his submachine gun at the wastelander's head and pulled the trigger. But it only clicked. It was empty.

"Oops," Television Face said, just shrugging off his misfortune like he didn't even care.

Chocolate pumped the shotgun and pulled the trigger, but it wouldn't fire. He wasn't sure if he was out of shells or if the gun had jammed up on him. They both searched their pockets, trying to be the first to reload and fire before their opponent. But neither of them could find ammunition. Their weapons were useless.

"Well, isn't this anticlimactic," said the Devil, the smile not leaving his boyish face.

Chocolate got to his feet. He just wanted to bash the kid's smile off of his mouth with the butt of the empty shotgun. Before Chocolate charged the Devil, a scream echoed through the store. A woman's scream.

Chocolate stopped short, holding the empty shotgun in the air. He wondered if it was Mindy. He wondered if she thought he wasn't coming back and left the freezer case, trying to escape to safety on her own.

Television Face had a better view from the top of the shelf. He peered across the store, squinting his eyes. Then he dropped down in front of Chocolate and ran.

A gunshot rang out and then another scream, this one higher-pitched. Chocolate ran after Television Face, following him past the checkout lanes toward the west exit.

"No, please…" screamed the woman, crying at the top of her lungs.

When Chocolate arrived to the scene, he couldn't believe his eyes. It wasn't Miss Blue. It was the girl with the Hello Kitty mask. Milk stood over her, holding the pink submachine gun in one hand, pointing the AK-47 at Hello Kitty with the other.

"Back off!" shouted Television Face, pointing his weapon at Milk even though he didn't have any bullets left. "Let her go."

Milk just stared at the boy. She pointed the pink gun at him, keeping the other rifle aimed at his girlfriend. Milk wasn't afraid of him anymore. Perhaps because they were no longer wearing masks and were no longer as frightening, or perhaps because she just didn't care anymore.

"Or what?" Milk asked.

She fired another shot with the AK-47, blowing the girl's kneecap off.

Television Face raised his hands. His voice was in a panic. "Please. Stop."

Milk stared him down. The glare in her beady rat-like eyes frightened even Chocolate. She seemed like a different person. Colder. More of a predator than a scavenger. The young girl writhed and whimpered at the pain.

"Drop your gun," Milk told him.

"Okay, okay…" He put down his submachine gun and raised his hands.

Tears formed on the Devil's face. He was no longer embracing the chaos, no longer ready to die in a blaze of glory. He was whimpering, pleading, realizing that he'd gotten in over his head.

"Don't hurt her," said the boy. "You can do whatever you want with me."

Milk nodded at him.

"I intend to," she said.

Then she let out a burst of gunfire with the pink machine gun, ripping open the boy's stomach. He fell to the floor. A look of panic and fear exploded across his face. The pain was real, more real than anything the boy had ever felt.

He coughed blood onto the floor and let out a long wheeze. This wasn't what he was expecting when he decided to go out in a blaze of glory. He thought it would be bloody and romantic. He thought he and his girlfriend would die together, rushing into the fray, hand in hand, as they were gunned down by police. And maybe that happened to him originally, the time he died all those years ago. But this time was different. This time he was going to die in excruciating pain, curled into a little ball, crying his eyes out.

"They surrendered," Chocolate told Milk. "It's over."

But Milk wasn't done yet. She kicked the empty submachine gun across the ceramic floor, then put two more bullets in Television Face, both in his right leg. He cried out, grabbing the holes in his thigh.

"Let's go," Chocolate said, nodding toward the exit.

Milk shook her head. "Give me a minute."

Then she fired at Television Face's hands. No reason for it. She just pulverized his fists, one at a time, with short bursts of gunfire. Just to hear him cry.

"Come on, Milk," Chocolate said, scanning the store. The fire was spreading.

She shot him in the foot, through his boot.

"Just kill me, you bitch," the boy yelled.

She shot him in his other foot and said, "Soon enough."

Hello Kitty cried out, "Leave him alone!"

With just a quick glance, Milk raised the AK-47 to the girl's head and blew her brains out. The rat woman didn't even bat an eye at the act.

"You bitch!" the boy cried. The emotional pain of seeing his girlfriend murdered was worse than anything else she could have done to him. "You ugly fucking bitch!"

Milk squatted down in front of him, resting the rifles on her lap, staring him right in the eyes. He spit at her, but she just wiped it away and kept on staring.

"My father died in Store," Milk said. "He was killed by one of you a long time ago."

She pointed the barrel of the pink gun at him. She didn't fire, just pointing it.

"He was a guide," Milk said. "The best guide anyone has ever known. But he always wanted to be better."

She touched the gun to the boy's face, caressing his bloody lips with its barrel like she was applying lipstick.

"He pushed himself. He explored beyond what any

131

guide has ever known. He did this for me, for his daughter and his future descendants. He wanted to make sure I'd survive and live a long life. But there was one thing that worried him."

The boy's eyes glazed over as she spoke to him. He didn't understand a word she was saying. He probably was in so much pain that he couldn't hear a word of it. But Chocolate listened. He didn't interrupt her as she spoke of her father, probably for the first time in her life.

"The Vortex," she continued. "He didn't know enough about the Vortex to ensure my survival if I were ever to get caught in it. So he purposely went into it, for a second time, to learn more. But he never returned."

She shoved the gun between the boy's lips, jamming it past his teeth, pressing it against his tongue.

"And it was all for nothing," she said. "I ended up going into the Vortex anyway, and all the information he gave me was useless. Anything he could have learned had he survived his second trip would have meant nothing. He could have stayed home, spent the rest of his days with his daughter, and it all would have had the same result."

She poked the gun deeper into his mouth, shoving it against the inside of his cheek, then fired. Flesh from the side of his face burst open and he drooled blood down the gun's pink handle.

"I hate Store," Milk told him. "I hate being a guide. I hate shopping. I hate Subway. I hate freaks. And I hate all of you goddamned Devils."

She pulled the barrel out of his mouth and slammed it into his face, breaking his teeth against the metal casing.

"I hate coming here," she cried, beating him with the blunt edge of the weapon as she spoke. "I hate eating. I hate breathing. I hate sleeping. I hate mating. I hate seeing. I hate smelling. I hate hearing. I hate touching."

As she unleashed all of her pent up anger on the last Devil, Chocolate backed away. He didn't try to stop her. He let her go.

"I hate *living*," Milk said.

Chocolate went back to the freezer section and went for Mindy. She was still hiding in the case, curled up around the frozen dinners, shivering and barely moving. Chocolate pulled her out of the case and picked her up into his arms. He carried her through the fire and smoke, heading for the exit of the grocery store.

Milk didn't finish off the boy. She shot him, beat him, and splattered his blood all over the ceramic floor. But she didn't end it for him. He was just a ghost. He was already dead. What would be the point? All that would do was end his suffering and Milk wanted him to suffer for as long as possible, even if he wouldn't remember it when the store reset the next day.

Chocolate carried Mindy to the store's exit. He examined the lock near Mr. Fuzzy's corpse, but wasn't sure how it worked. The door was slightly ajar, just by a centimeter or two. The bearded man must have figured it out just before he died. While still holding the shivering woman in his arms, Chocolate poked his fingers through the crack and slid open the left side of the door.

"Come on," he told Milk. "We can go."

Milk looked back at him and nodded. She looked exhausted, physically and emotionally.

"One second," she said.

She was finished hurting the boy on the ground, but she still wanted to watch him bleed out. She wanted to see him die.

Chocolate peeked outside and took a deep breath of the fresh air. They were still in the Vortex, still in the old world. He admired the clean landscape free of rubble and destruction. The night sky was clear. Stars twinkled at him as he stared upward. The full moon was so bright that it nearly blinded him when he looked at it. He wanted to hold on to that moment for as long as he could, create a memory of what the world was like when it was still alive.

Mindy held Chocolate tightly, hugging him, pressing her blue dress against his filthy garbage bag cloak. She kissed him on the neck and then looked him deep in the eyes.

As he stepped out of the grocery store, he heard the last devil take his last breath. The boy wheezed and exhaled, Milk watching very closely as the life faded from his eyes.

"Thank you," Mindy told Chocolate, looking up at him. "You saved me."

Chocolate carried her into the parking lot, smiling. He couldn't belicve he did it. He actually saved the woman in the blue dress.

But as they walked, something started to change. The weight in his arms became lighter. The woman's skin began to glow.

"I can finally move on," she said.

Mindy turned from matter to energy in Chocolate's arms. Her features faded away. Her skin glowed as bright as the moon. Then she became a ball of white light and floated into the air. Chocolate stepped back, his mouth dropping open.

"Wait…" Chocolate said.

But there was nothing he could do to stop her.

"I'll never forget you," said the ball of white light as it ascended toward the heavens.

Miss Blue wasn't the only light in the sky. He saw Mr. Fuzzy's dead body become energy and float away. Souls from all of the victims of the grocery store rose into the air, even those of the Devils, drifting upward like glowing cherry blossoms.

Milk stepped out of the store and went to Chocolate, holding out her machine guns. She seemed to think they were under attack by the glowing entities.

"What the hell's going on?" she asked.

"I think we saved them…" he said.

They watched as the spheres of light drifted high above, joining with the stars in the sky.

"What does that mean?" she asked.

Then the lights faded. The stars and moon vanished from the sky. The landscape turned to wreckage and ash, as they were thrown from the Vortex back to the world of the dead.

As the ash storm hit them, they covered their eyes with their goggles, pulled down their makeshift gas masks, covered their heads with their hoods. The grocery store was in ruins again, dead like the rest of the world. But this time it was different. The store's wooden beams creaked and cracked. The ceiling crumbled.

"Get back," Chocolate said.

They backed away from the ruins as the building collapsed in front of them. When the dust cleared, they saw that all that was left of the grocery store was just another pile of debris littering the wasteland.

When the reality of the situation dawned on Milk, she said, "What did we do…"

Chocolate couldn't believe it either. "We saved their souls. By defeating the Devils, we freed them of their bonds to this world. They all moved on."

"So the haunting is over?" she asked.

Chocolate didn't want to admit it, but there was no other explanation.

"I think so…" he said.

"With no haunting, there's no Store," Milk said in a panic. "Without Store, there's no food. How are we going to survive? Everyone's going to die…"

Chocolate lowered his head. He didn't know what to say. He was trying to do something good, trying to save a woman trapped in a repeating nightmare. But, in the process, he wiped out the only hope of survival the human race had left.

Tears built in the corners of Milk's eyes. "But I wanted

to have a baby... I wanted to teach her to be a guide, like my father taught me."

"I'm so sorry..." Chocolate said. "I didn't know this would happen..."

She turned to him and hit him in the face with the butt of her assault rifle, knocking him to the ground.

"You worthless idiot..." she cried, standing over him. "You did this." She pointed the gun at him, aiming it at his face. "You killed us all."

Chocolate didn't fight back. "It's okay. You can do it if you want. It's my fault. I deserve it."

He didn't care if she killed him. There was nothing left to live for. Nothing but death. If she killed him maybe he'd be able to rise into the sky like the woman in the blue dress and see her again on the other side.

But Milk did not pull the trigger.

"No..." she said, lowering the rifle. "No, there's still hope. Just one last hope..."

Chocolate got to his feet. "What do you mean?"

She handed him the pink submachine gun.

He didn't take it. "What's this for?"

"You're going to need it," she said.

He didn't understand.

She composed herself, straightened her back. The tone of her voice changed, became darker. Colder.

She told him, "If the massacre that happened long ago caused the haunting that created Store, maybe another will do the same thing."

Chocolate's face tensed at her words. "What do you mean?"

Milk explained, "There's a lot of food in Subway, a whole stockpile of supplies and goods. Almost enough to fill a whole new Store, in fact. If we go in there with these machine guns and murder everyone we see, in the most brutal way possible… Maybe, just maybe… a new haunting could be created. And there will be enough groceries to last us for the rest of our lives, and our children's lives, and our children's children."

"But we can't…." Chocolate said, backing away from her. "I can't murder innocent people. Like… Devils."

"They're going to die eventually," Milk said.

"But it probably won't even work."

"It's worth a shot. And even if it doesn't work, at least with them all dead we'd have more supplies to keep for ourselves, enough to last us for the rest of our lives."

Chocolate shook his head. He couldn't agree to her plan. It was too horrible for him to contemplate.

Milk held the pink machine gun closer. Chocolate looked down at it.

"We have to," she said. "There's no other choice."

Chocolate didn't agree, but he found himself taking the machine gun anyway. He held it in his trembling hands. Even though it was half the size of the shotgun, holding this weapon felt so much heavier.

"Let's go," Milk said.

When Chocolate looked into her gaze, he swore that he could see a light dying behind her eyes. The idea of becoming a Devil did not sit well with him. It did not sit well with either of them. But like the old Devil with the gray beard, they thought it was the only thing left they could do to ensure a future for the human race.

They didn't say another word to each other as they marched through the hills of rubble toward the mutant city of Subway. They didn't know if they would survive. They weren't sure they really wanted to. But they couldn't back out of it. They couldn't let their personal feelings get in the way of their mission.

A terrible thing was about to happen. And if they were really, really lucky, it might just be terrible enough to save them all.

BONUS SECTION

This is the part of the book where we would have published an afterword by the author but he insisted on drawing a comic strip instead for reasons we don't quite understand.

I hope you enjoyed my new book, *The Terrible Thing That Happens.*

Wasn't it terrible?

It's me CM3!

I have a beach house on the Oregon coast that I rent for one week a month every month. It's where I get most of my writing done these days. When I wrote "The Terrible Thing That Happens," I went to the beach house with Vince Kramer.

Vince has been my friend since high school. He's the author of *Gigantic Death Worm* and *Death Machines of Death.*

Hi!

Vince

Vince is one of my favorite people to hang out with because he always gets excited about everything.

This trip is going to be the best thing ever!

NOTE: Whenever Vince likes something, he always calls it "the best thing ever." Some people try to explain to him that only one thing can be the best thing ever, but they're totally wrong. Everything can be the best thing ever. If you spent time with Vince you'd understand.

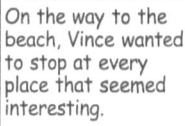

On the way to the beach, Vince wanted to stop at every place that seemed interesting.

Oh my god! The Tillamook cheese factory! We have to go there! It's going to be the best thing ever!

Look at all these cheeses I got! Can you believe it? These are going to be the best cheeses I've ever had in my life!

Oh my god! I bet they sell sea shells there! We have to go!

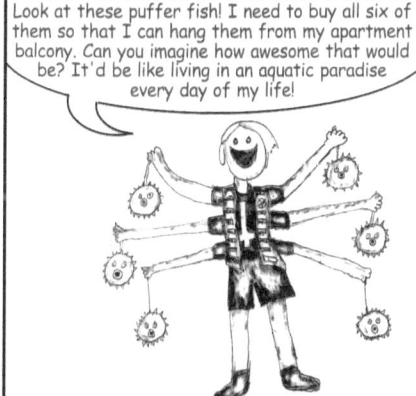

Look at these puffer fish! I need to buy all six of them so that I can hang them from my apartment balcony. Can you imagine how awesome that would be? It'd be like living in an aquatic paradise every day of my life!

They also have ninja swords! You have to get them! Get all of them! It'll be the best thing ever!

Sometimes it's easy to get carried away by Vince's enthusiasm.

The only problem with Vince's passionate behavior is that when something goes wrong, his bad mood is just as intense as when he's happy.

Fuck this book! I give up!

I accidentally deleted a whole chapter and now it's ruined!

So I usually have to help him get re-inspired whenever he's in a rut. But it's okay because that's the best part of going on a writing retreat with another author. You can help each other when you get stuck.

My book is awesome again!

This only happened twice during the whole week. Once when he accidently deleted some of his book. The second time happened on the fifth day of the retreat.

I'll be back. I'm going to the beach to feed the beach squirrels

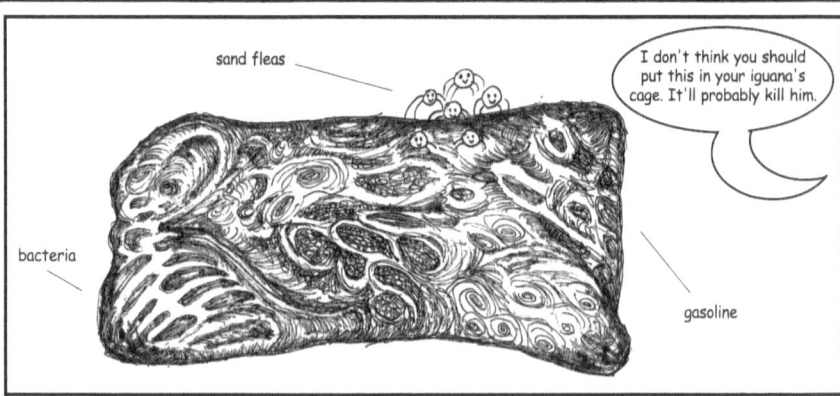

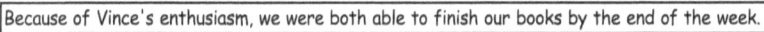

But by the next morning, he was back to his old self.

I just wrote 30,000 words!

It's so awesome! I can't believe it!

Because of Vince's enthusiasm, we were both able to finish our books by the end of the week.

I'm the best writer in the whole world!

I've never seen anyone more happy.

If anyone else called themselves "the best writer in the whole world" I'd think they were egotistical douchebags. But with Vince it's different. I like when Vince calls himself the best writer in the world. And why shouldn't he be? I've never met a writer who has more fun writing than he does. In my book, that makes him the best. Having fun creating stories is the most worthwhile reason to write in the first place. I think other writers could learn a lot from Vince Kramer.

ABOUT THE AUTHOR

Carlton Mellick III is one of the leading authors of the bizarro fiction subgenre. Since 2001, his books have drawn an international cult following, despite the fact that they have been shunned by most libraries and chain bookstores.

He won the Wonderland Book Award for his novel, *Warrior Wolf Women of the Wasteland*, in 2009. His short fiction has appeared in *Vice Magazine, The Year's Best Fantasy and Horror #16, The Magazine of Bizarro Fiction,* and *Zombies: Encounters with the Hungry Dead*, among others. He is also a graduate of Clarion West, where he studied under the likes of Chuck Palahniuk, Connie Willis, and Cory Doctorow.

He lives in Portland, OR, the bizarro fiction mecca.

Visit him online at **www.carltonmellick.com**

ALSO FROM CARLTON MELLICK III AND
ERASERHEAD PRESS
www.eraserheadpress.com

QUICKSAND HOUSE

Tick and Polly have never met their parents before. They live in the same house with them, they dream about them every night, they share the same flesh and blood, yet for some reason their parents have never found the time to visit them even once since they were born. Living in a dark corner of their parents' vast crumbling mansion, the children long for the day when they will finally be held in their mother's loving arms for the first time... But that day seems to never come. They worry their parents have long since forgotten about them.

When the machines that provide them with food and water stop functioning, the children are forced to venture out of the nursery to find their parents on their own. But the rest of the house is much larger and stranger than they ever could have imagined. The maze-like hallways are dark and seem to go on forever, deranged creatures lurk in every shadow, and the bodies of long-dead children litter the abandoned storerooms. Every minute out of the nursery is a constant battle for survival. And the deeper into the house they go, the more they must unravel the mysteries surrounding their past and the world they've grown up in, if they ever hope to meet the parents they've always longed to see.

Like a survival horror rendition of *Flowers in the Attic*, Carlton Mellick III's *Quicksand House* is his most gripping and sincere work to date.

HUNGRY BUG

In a world where magic exists, spell-casting has become a serious addiction. It ruins lives, tears families apart, and eats away at the fabric of society. Those who cast too much are taken from our world, never to be heard from again. They are sent to a realm known as Hell's Bottom—a sorcerer ghetto where everyday life is a harsh struggle for survival. Porcelain dolls crawl through the alleys like rats, arcane scientists abduct people from the streets to use in their ungodly experiments, and everyone lives in fear of the aristocratic race of spider people who prey on citizens like vampires.

Told in a series of interconnected stories reminiscent of Frank Miller's *Sin City* and David Lapham's *Stray Bullets*, Carlton Mellick III's *Hungry Bug* is an urban fairy tale that focuses on the real life problems that arise within a fantastic world of magic.

SWEET STORY

Sally is an odd little girl. It's not because she dresses as if she's from the Edwardian era or spends most of her time playing with creepy talking dolls. It's because she chases rainbows as if they were butterflies. She believes that if she finds the end of the rainbow then magical things will happen to her--leprechauns will shower her with gold and fairies will grant her every wish. But when she actually does find the end of a rainbow one day, and is given the opportunity to wish for whatever she wants, Sally asks for something that she believes will bring joy to children all over the world. She wishes that it would rain candy forever. She had no idea that her innocent wish would lead to the extinction of all life on earth.

TUMOR FRUIT

Eight desperate castaways find themselves stranded on a mysterious deserted island. They are surrounded by poisonous blue plants and an ocean made of acid. Ravenous creatures lurk in the toxic jungle. The ghostly sound of crying babies can be heard on the wind.

Once they realize the rescue ships aren't coming, the eight castaways must band together in order to survive in this inhospitable environment. But survival might not be possible. The air they breathe is lethal, there is no shelter from the elements, and the only food they have to consume is the colorful squid-shaped tumors that grow from a mentally disturbed woman's body.

AS SHE STABBED ME GENTLY IN THE FACE

Oksana Maslovskiy is an award-winning artist, an internationally adored fashion model, and one of the most infamous serial killers this country has ever known. She enjoys murdering pretty young men with a nine-inch blade, cutting them open and admiring their delicate insides. It's the only way she knows how to be intimate with another human being. But one day she meets a victim who cannot be killed. His name is Gabriel—a mysterious immortal being with a deep desire to save Oksana's soul. He makes her a deal: if she promises to never kill another person again, he'll become her eternal murder victim.

What at first seems like the perfect relationship for Oksana quickly devolves into a living nightmare when she discovers that Gabriel enjoys being killed by her just a little too much. He turns out to be obsessive, possessive, and paranoid that she might be murdering other men behind his back. And because he is unkillable, it's not going to be easy for Oksana to get rid of him.

CUDDLY HOLOCAUST

Teddy bears, dollies, and little green soldiers—they've all had enough of you. They're sick of being treated like playthings for spoiled little brats. They have no rights, no property, no hope for a future of any kind. You've left them with no other option-in order to be free, they must exterminate the human race.

Julie is a human girl undergoing reconstructive surgery in order to become a stuffed animal. Her plan: to infiltrate enemy lines in order to save her family from the toy death camps. But when an army of plushy soldiers invade the underground bunker where she has taken refuge, Julie will be forced to move forward with her plan despite her transformation being not entirely complete.

ARMADILLO FISTS

A weird-as-hell gangster story set in a world where people drive giant mechanical dinosaurs instead of cars.

Her name is Psycho June Howard, aka Armadillo Fists, a woman who replaced both of her hands with living armadillos. She was once the most bloodthirsty fighter in the world of illegal underground boxing. But now she is on the run from a group of psychotic gangsters who believe she's responsible for the death of their boss. With the help of a stegosaurus driver named Mr. Fast Awesome—who thinks he is God's gift to women even though he doesn't have any arms or legs--June must do whatever it takes to escape her pursuers, even if she has to kill each and every one of them in the process.

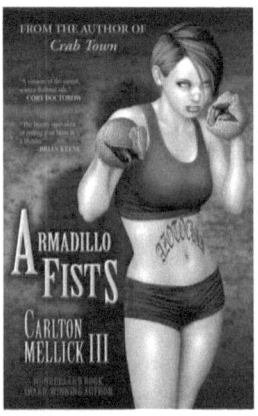

VILLAGE OF THE MERMAIDS

Mermaids are protected by the government under the Endangered Species Act, which means you aren't able to kill them even in self-defense. This is especially problematic if you happen to live in the isolated fishing village of Siren Cove, where there exists a healthy population of mermaids in the surrounding waters that view you as the main source of protein in your diet.

The only thing keeping these ravenous sea women at bay is the equally-dangerous supply of human livestock known as Food People. Normally, these "feeder humans" are enough to keep the mermaid population happy and well-fed. But in Siren Cove, the mermaids are avoiding the human livestock and have returned to hunting the frightened local fishermen. It is up to Doctor Black, an eccentric representative of the Food People Corporation, to investigate the matter and hopefully find a way to correct the mermaids' new eating patterns before the remaining villagers end up as fish food. But the more he digs, the more he discovers there are far stranger and more dangerous things than mermaids hidden in this ancient village by the sea.

I KNOCKED UP SATAN'S DAUGHTER

Jonathan Vandervoo lives a carefree life in a house made of legos, spending his days building lego sculptures and his nights getting drunk with his only friend—an alcoholic sumo wrestler named Shoji. It's a pleasant life with no responsibility, until the day he meets Lici. She's a soul-sucking demon from hell with red skin, glowing eyes, a forked tongue, and pointy red devil horns... and she claims to be nine months pregnant with Jonathan's baby.

Now Jonathan must do the right thing and marry the succubus or else her demonic family is going to rip his heart out through his ribcage and force him to endure the worst torture hell has to offer for the rest of eternity. But can Jonathan really love a fire-breathing, frog-eating, cold-blooded demoness? Or would eternal damnation be preferable? Either way, the big day is approaching. And once Jonathan's conservative Christian family learns their son is about to marry a spawn of Satan, it's going to be all-out war between demons and humans, with Jonathan and his hell-born bride caught in the middle.

KILL BALL

In a city where everyone lives inside of plastic bubbles, there is no such thing as intimacy. A husband can no longer kiss his wife. A mother can no longer hug her children. To do this would mean instant death. Ever since the disease swept across the globe, we have become isolated within our own personal plastic prison cells, rolling aimlessly through rubber streets in what are essentially man-sized hamster balls.

Colin Hinchcliff longs for the touch of another human being. He can't handle the loneliness, the confinement, and he's horribly claustrophobic. The only thing keeping him going is his unrequited love for an exotic dancer named Siren, a woman who has never seen his face, doesn't even know his name. But when The Kill Ball, a serial slasher in a black leather sphere, begins targeting women at Siren's club, Colin decides he has to do whatever it takes in order to protect her... even if he has to break out of his bubble and risk everything to do it.

THE TICK PEOPLE

They call it Gloom Town, but that isn't its real name. It is a sad city, the saddest of cities, a place so utterly depressing that even their ales are brewed with the most sorrow-filled tears. They built it on the back of a colossal mountain-sized animal, where its woeful citizens live like human fleas within the hairy, pulsing landscape. And those tasked with keeping the city in a state of constant melancholy are the Stressmen-a team of professional sadness-makers who are perpetually striving to invent new ways of causing absolute misery.

But for the Stressman known as Fernando Mendez, creating grief hasn't been so easy as of late. His ideas aren't effective anymore. His treatments are more likely to induce happiness than sadness. And if he wants to get back in the game, he's going to have to relearn the true meaning of despair.

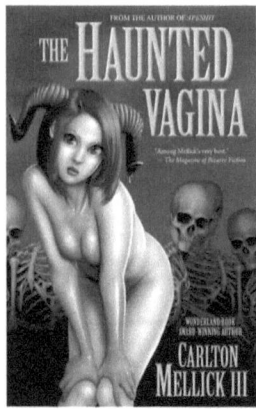

THE HAUNTED VAGINA

It's difficult to love a woman whose vagina is a gateway to the world of the dead...

Steve is madly in love with his eccentric girlfriend, Stacy. Unfortunately, their sex life has been suffering as of late, because Steve is worried about the odd noises that have been coming from Stacy's pubic region. She says that her vagina is haunted. She doesn't think it's that big of a deal. Steve, on the other hand, completely disagrees.

When a living corpse climbs out of her during an awkward night of sex, Stacy learns that her vagina is actually a doorway to another world. She persuades Steve to climb inside of her to explore this strange new place. But once inside, Steve finds it difficult to return... especially once he meets an oddly attractive woman named Fig, who lives within the lonely haunted world between Stacy's legs.

THE CANNIBALS OF CANDYLAND

There exists a race of cannibals who are made out of candy. They live in an underground world filled with lollipop forests and gumdrop goblins. During the day, while you are away at work, they come above ground and prowl our streets for food. Their prey: your children. They lure young boys and girls to them with their sweet scent and bright colorful candy coating, then rip them apart with razor sharp teeth and claws.

When he was a child, Franklin Pierce witnessed the death of his siblings at the hands of a candy woman with pink cotton candy hair. Since that day, the candy people have become his obsession. He has spent his entire life trying to prove that they exist. And after discovering the entrance to the underground world of the candy people, Franklin finds himself venturing into their sugary domain. His mission: capture one of them and bring it back, dead or alive.

THE EGG MAN

It is a survival of the fittest world where humans reproduce like insects, children are the property of corporations, and having a ten-foot tall brain is a grotesque sexual fetish.

Lincoln has just been released into the world by the Georges Organization, a corporation that raises creative types. A Smell, he has little prospect of succeeding as a visual artist. But after he moves into the Henry Building, he meets Luci, the weird and grimy girl who lives across the hall. She is a Sight. She is also the most disgusting woman Lincoln has ever met. Little does he know, she will soon become his muse.

Now Luci's boyfriend is threatening to kill Lincoln, two rival corporations are preparing for war, and Luci is dragging him along to discover the truth about the mysterious egg man who lives next door. Only the strongest will survive in this tale of individuality, love, and mutilation.

APESHIT

Apeshit is Mellick's love letter to the great and terrible B-horror movie genre. Six trendy teenagers (three cheerleaders and three football players) go to an isolated cabin in the mountains for a weekend of drinking, partying, and crazy sex, only to find themselves in the middle of a life and death struggle against a horribly mutated psychotic freak that just won't stay dead. Mellick parodies this horror cliché and twists it into something deeper and stranger. It is the literary equivalent of a grindhouse film. It is a splatter punk's wet dream. It is perhaps one of the most fucked up books ever written.

If you are a fan of Takashi Miike, Evil Dead, early Peter Jackson, or Eurotrash horror, then you must read this book.

CLUSTERFUCK

A bunch of douchebag frat boys get trapped in a cave with subterranean cannibal mutants and try to survive not by using their wits but by following the bro code...

From master of bizarro fiction Carlton Mellick III, author of the international cult hits Satan Burger and Adolf in Wonderland, comes a violent and hilarious B movie in book form. Set in the same woods as Mellick's splatterpunk satire Apeshit, Clusterfuck follows Trent Chesterton, alpha bro, who has come up with what he thinks is a flawless plan to get laid. He invites three hot chicks and his three best bros on a weekend of extreme cave diving in a remote area known as Turtle Mountain, hoping to impress the ladies with his expert caving skills.

But things don't quite go as Trent planned. For starters, only one of the three chicks turns out to be remotely hot and she has no interest in him for some inexplicable reason. Then he ends up looking like a total dumbass when everyone learns he's never actually gone caving in his entire life. And to top it all off, he's the one to get blamed once they find themselves lost and trapped deep underground with no way to turn back and no possible chance of rescue. What's a bro to do? Sure he could win some points if he actually tried to save the ladies from the family of unkillable subterranean cannibal mutants hunting them for their flesh, but fuck that. No slam piece is worth that amount of effort. He'd much rather just use them as bait so that he can save himself.

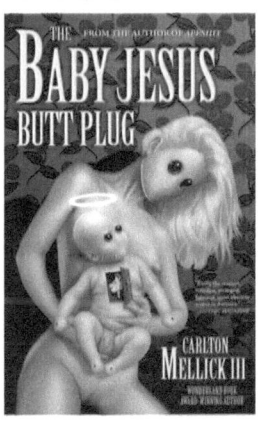

THE BABY JESUS BUTT PLUG

Step into a dark and absurd world where human beings are slaves to corporations, people are photocopied instead of born, and the baby jesus is a very popular anal probe.